I WON'T LOSE TO LOVE AGAIN

IESHA BREE

Synopsis

Alena has survived one too many failed relationships, and this time around she has no intentions on allowing love to win again, especially after her last relationship ended terribly. When she meets Nash, an NBA player with qualities that no woman can deny and a fighting spirit, she just might be ready to play the game of love once more, but there are unknown problems waiting to come her way. Will love continue to have the last laugh, or will she prevail?

Two best friends couldn't be more similar. As Alena struggles to avoid love and keep her studio running smooth, Lavonka, who has had her fair share of love lost, meets Bronx, who has the potential to be her true love. But will exes and secrets that come back to haunt their relationship threaten the bond they have worked so hard to build? Will Lavonka and Alena learn that they can finally have their happy ending without thinking everything is just too good to be true? Take a ride with these two women from Florida to see who will be on the winning end of love.

Acknowledgement/ Dedications

I want to first dedicate this book to God because without him, this would not be possible, and then to my family whose support is endless. I also want to thank my good friend Kenya (Model) and Rick Crank (Photographer) for allowing me to use her as the model for my cover, which she was perfect for if I might add! Last but not least, I can't forget my girls Asia Monique & C. Monet for encouraging me to finish this book and for their support!

To my readers, I know we started this out with the Mae sisters, and I'm excited for the new journey we will continue with these new sets of characters. I also appreciate all the support and comments you leave me! Without y'all, I wouldn't be able to grow into the author I am becoming, so I appreciate y'all!

Thanks for giving me a chance, and reading my versions of love.

"So, tell me why I got a call from Trina telling me she saw yo' man out with some toothpick looking ass bitch!" Lavonka yelled through the phone.

"Who man?" I asked because my man was at work. Shoot, at least that's what his dumb ass told me.

"I know you can hear! Girl, yo' man, big headed Quran, is out with some pool stick looking bitch."

I swear this girl was always yelling, but in this situation, I was going to make an exception because he had me entirely fucked up.

"Come get me. We can't go in my car. He is going to recognize it!" I responded, throwing on my sneakers and tying my hair back into a bun. I heard a horn honking; she was forever honking that damn horn and trying to wake up all my damn neighbors.

"Bring yo' ass on! I got the address. Let's hurry up before his ass tries to leave thinking he about to be finding his way through the desert!" she yelled as I got into the car.

"Girl, ain't no desert over here! We in Florida!" I laughed because I knew exactly what she was talking about, but this chick just cracked me up.

"Well, Quran is going to be the first man in history to find a desert right in the middle of Florida between a pair of stick legs!" she yelled, bursting out into laughter because she knew just as much as I did how foolish she was.

"Girl, please!" We laughed as she turned up the radio and "Get Money" from Junior Mafia started playing just as Lil' Kim's part started. Lavonka and I started rapping like we were going through the same shit.

"Break up affairs, lick shots in the air, You get vexed and start swinging everywhere. Me shifty? Now you wanna pistol whip me." We went back and forth until the part we had been waiting for to get us hyped up to pop up on this nigga came. *"Is you with me? How could you ever deceive me? But paybacks a bitch, motherfucker, believe me."*

By the time we rapped that last verse, we were pulling up to this little restaurant. This muthafucka ain't never took me to no restaurant like this, but he could take chopstick looking bitches.

"Vonka, you smaller than me. Get out, go get in that bush, and tell me if you see that nigga!" I whispered as we squatted down next to her car.

"Oh, hell no, Lena. This is yo' cheating ass man. What I look like getting in a damn bush!" She snapped her neck to look at me like I had lost my mind.

"Man, he gonna see me if I go!" I whispered back with a pleading voice.

"Ain't that the damn point? He needs to know you saw him out being a dumbass. We ain't drive over here to watch a damn movie! I came to whoop ass!" she snapped, still not budging on getting in that bush as I began to pout, which I knew would get her to do it.

"Ugh, damn alright! But you owe me!"

"Getting in some damn bush like I'm Inspector Gadget or some shit. Get on my nerves," I heard her mumble as I laughed.

I knew she was going to talk shit, but at the end of the day, she was always gon' have my back, I thought as I watched her squat down behind the bush to get a better view. I knew she saw Quran's lying ass when she went to grab her gun out the back of her pants but forgot she left it in the car. I ran to squat down as low as I could as I got to the same bush she was behind.

"Let's go. I know you saw his ass," I whispered.

"You ain't said nothing but a word, but his Squid-ward looking ass better be glad I left my gun in the car. I would have shot his ass on principle alone," she responded, looking around us to check our surroundings.

I laughed because I knew she wasn't playing, which was precisely why I was happy she left it in the car. *We were not going to jail tonight*, I thought as we stepped up from behind the bush and hopped over the railing of the patio. We started to make our way toward the table he was seated at with some dumb looking ass bitch. I knew the minute he saw us because Quran looked as if he wanted to get up and run and leave her ass there. I laughed as Vonka and I grabbed chairs from the surrounding tables to have a seat with them while his new bitch looked at us like she was ready to explode. The waiter walked up just in time for us to order as well.

"So, will you ladies be joining them?" he asked with a polite smile while looking at Lavonka and me like we were breakfast, lunch, and dinner.

I looked over at Quran to notice he was getting pissed off, but I couldn't care less. Like me, Lavonka said yes, and his bitch had the nerve to cut us off while we were ordering our drinks with an attitude.

"Uh, excuse you, you're at the wrong table. Me and my man are trying to have a nice dinner, thank you. Now, have a nice day. I'm sure he can escort you to your correct table," she added in a snippy tone.

Where in the hell did he find this bitch? I smiled back as Lavonka looked over at me as we burst out laughing at this girl.

She didn't realize how close she was to getting her ass beat. I was trying to have a little sympathy for her. *I was sure this nigga didn't tell her he had a loving and beautiful as fuck girlfriend at home, whose pussy just couldn't wait to drown him the minute he got home. I was sure he missed all of those details by the way she popped off, but she had one more time, and I was gonna be on her ass like white on rice, trust and believe that,* I thought as I straightened out my clothes and ignored her.

"So, Quran, we not invited? Normally, when a nigga see his girl, he at least hops up to feel on her ass or something?" I asked as I tilted my head to the side with a smile as I watched him try to formulate a bunch of bullshit that I wasn't in the mood to hear.

"Well, you know what? I'm only going to say this one time and one time only, you really got me fucked up! Once you leave this funky ass date, don't even think about stepping foot on our porch, 'kay?" I added as the waiter came with both Lavonka's and my shot of Henny. We quickly threw them back and hopped out of our seats to leave.

I heard Ms. Bougie say something along the lines of "I'm glad those ghetto bitches are leaving, and what the hell was that fat one talking about?" If there was anything I didn't tolerate was anybody calling me out of my name and talking about the size of my body. I didn't consider myself fat, but I was definitely on the thicker side with the thick thighs fat ass and all. My body was built to be taken on a ride all night with the face of an angel, if I might say so myself. But don't let my sweet and innocent smile fool you, I was not the one. I turned around as Quran hopped out of his chair, because he knew just like I did what was about to go down. I reached over the table and dragged her ass over the table, knocking glasses and plates over along with her. I began to show her how much of a ghetto fat bitch I was when I felt Lavonka grabbing me and telling me the cops were coming.

"Try me again like that!" I yelled as we left the scene, hopped in the car, and sped off.

"I thought you were going to kill that little girl!" Vonka yelled while laughing. I was still mad as hell, but

I could at least laugh at the situation, but come tomorrow, I knew he was going to be on that shit acting like I overacted or something, and I was just tired of it.

After going for drinks, I finally got to my house and Quran was sleeping in the back room like I didn't tell his ass not to come home, but that was all right. *He was going to find out tomorrow*, I thought as I grabbed a throw blanket out of my closet and headed to the guest bedroom.

Next day

"Who you on the phone with, Alena? You know I don't play that shit. Who you talking to whispering and shit!" Quran yelled, causing me to flinch, because anytime he got this riled up, he was ready to fight. I wasn't a weak ass a woman, so we would be rolling all around this bitch if he decided to act stupid today. I was tired of the fighting.

"Lavonka! Damn, why you all in my conversation? Why don't you ask that bitch you were fucking that kept you out all last night about her whereabouts—" I yelled when I felt his hand fly across my face.

My hand instantly went to my cheek as if that was going to make the sting from his hand connecting to my face disappear. I instantly began to nod my head and looked his way. I could see his lips moving and automatically knew he was talking shit, but I was so damn mad, my ass went deaf for a minute. I didn't say anything else to him. I didn't even try to fight back. I was just tired, so I turned on my heels and headed toward our room in the back of the house, snatched my bags out of the closet, and started to pack my shit.

If he thought for one minute that I was the type of bitch to play with, he had lost his mind, I thought as I began to stuff everything I could get my hands on into my duffle bag while reaching for my Tiffany Blue Inspired Glock 43. I made sure it was loaded because I knew he wasn't just going to let me leave. When I heard knocking at the door, I knew without a doubt Lavonka was at the door ready to kick that door the hell down. Walking to the front, I could hear the game playing on the TV. *This muthafucka really had the nerve to hit me and then have a seat like shit didn't happened,* I thought while heading to the front with my stuff in hand and gun cocked ready to put his ass straight to sleep if he wanted to jump stupid.

"Where the hell you think—" he tried to ask before he heard the sound of me cocking my gun while backing toward the front door to let myself out.

"You ain't got to worry about that, because if you make one false move, your ass gonna be straight in hell before your time. Trust and believe that," I said in a tone that could have frozen over hell. When I reached the door, I opened it, and just like I expected, Lavonka was on the other side with her matching Glock 43 but in purple and black aimed at the door.

This was precisely why she was my girl. She was always down to ride, no matter the situation.

"I knew I should have been shot yo' ass! I told you he wasn't shit, Lena!" she yelled, cocking her gun because he hopped out of his seat and was getting ready to walk toward me until he heard the sound of Lavonka cocking her gun, which was smart because, although I was pissed, I didn't know if I could actually kill him. Now, Lavonka, on the other hand, wouldn't think twice about it. She would consider it self-defense, and Quran knew that.

"Babe, let's just talk about this without her. You know that wasn't me. I didn't mean to do that!" he stated, trying to sweet talk me.

At one point, I used to love the sounds of his voice, the feel of his hands, and the way his ass used to stroke my body into oblivion, but it was something about having a man with community dick and a fiery temper that made that shit not matter one bit.

"Fuck you! And don't you call me no more or come near me, because the next time you won't have to worry about there being a next time! Trust and believe that!" I yelled, backing out of the house with Lavonka on my heels. We had thrown my bags into her back seat and sped away from the house when the reality of the situation started to finally hit as we got on the highway to head to her home.

I knew she was speechless, because she knew I usually needed time to calm down whenever I got that angry. I was naturally the type of woman who felt as if you were supposed to treat your man like he was a king, and that when he needed you that you were always there. I would consider myself a ride or die type of chick, but at some point, I made them overly comfortable. When had it ever been a problem to be everything your man needed? But shit, if you asked me, it hadn't been working out too well. I had yet to be in a relationship with a man that had appreciated anything I'd done.

"I can't even believe I let myself repeat the same shit again!" I yelled more to myself than at Lavonka, breaking the silence.

"I don' told you that these niggas ain't good for shit but dick, and some of them can't even get that right! So what you think they gonna do when they run into a female like you? Trust me, you know I been there done that before. I know you remember Troy's cheating ass! He was on that same shit as Quran, but you see where his ass ended up," she stated in a sweet voice like it was an everyday occurrence that people just ended up in the hospital from cheating. But then again, Quran was getting ready to make a special appearance at Mercy Hospital.

I swear something was wrong with this woman, but it was alright. She always had my back, no matter how crazy her ass was!

"Girl, please. I don't know why you saying it like everybody ends up in the hospital when they fuck somebody over. If that's the case, we would all be some hospitalized muthafuckas." I laughed for the first time.

"Ain't nobody said nothing about the outcome. I'm talking about how he got there. You know I shot his ass," she added seriously.

I didn't even know why she brought this man up, because every time she did, her mood switched up just like the damn weather! One minute it was hot and the next cold.

"I swear you are so trigger happy." I laughed just thinking about that situation. I was surprised he never pressed charges on her crazy ass.

"I disagree. If I was so trigger happy, I would have shot Quran's big-headed ass right between his eyes, but as you can see, he gets to see another day," she added, throwing me a wink while turning back to focus on getting us to our destination.

I just shook my head, because there was no helping this woman. She just didn't have any sense.

We finally made it to her house. She lived in the boonies, if you asked me. She pulled her car into her driveway.

"Now you know you can stay here as long as you need to. Looks like we back roommates unless you got plan on making a trip back to Ike's house?" she asked with the most serious expression.

I was confused as all hell. Who in the hell was Ike? Then, I looked back up at her trying to hold in her smirk. "Ohhh, that Ike! Too early!" I laughed, finally catching on to what she was saying. But she knew like I did that, although I was a big romantic, I was nobody's punching bag.

I thought to myself as I grabbed my bags and headed to the front door. Although you would assume her ghetto ass wasn't living as well off as she was, my homegirl was extremely book smart. She was an accountant for the major league people in the business world before we decided to pursue our dreams of being background dancers. Having this big ol' house didn't attribute to just her wealth, she had been dating this sexy ass man named Bronx. He was a ballplayer that she met on one of our outings a year back. The way this chick acted you would never know she had a good man waiting right at home for her. I knew he was home as well when we walked past his all-black Rolls Royce sitting in the driveway, especially when Lavonka turned toward me and gave me a look not to say nothing about the situation because he was just as crazy as she was about me. We had become close, like a brother-sister relationship. I didn't connect well with anyone she dated but him, because I knew he had her best interest at heart, unlike Troy, who she used to mess with.

"Lena, don't say shit. I'm not in the mood for his mouth," she whispered when the door flew open.

"Nah, don't be out here doing all that whispering shit. Get in here. I don' called yo' ass a thousand times. Where was you at?" he asked not even noticing I was walking next to her. He finally looked my way and looked down at the bags I was carrying to give me a hand.

"Wassup, sis! I see you decided to leave that no-good ass nigga for real this time," he added while still looking at Lavonka, waiting for an answer that never came as she made her way past him and into the house.

I followed behind them into the house. I loved my girl, but sometimes she made shit harder for herself when all of this was unnecessary. I didn't give a damn about Bronx knowing, but if my girl wanted to keep it between us, I would.

"I know you hear me talking to you, Vee," he added while walking ahead of her to place my bags in my room as I shook my head and walked in behind him.

I watched him walk back out because Vonka still hadn't said anything as she proceeded to walk to their bedroom. I closed the door behind them as I laid back in the bed as the reality of the situation finally hit me. This man had put his hands on me. What did I have to do to be loved? I was tired of this bullshit. Every time I got into a relationship, it always ended badly.

EVERY TIME I CALLED MYSELF IN LOVE, LOVE PUT ME ON my ass and showed me I was unworthy to be in its presence. But this time, love would have me fucked up if it tried that shit again. I was just done with these fuck niggas and men in general until I figured out why I was unworthy. *Maybe I needed this time to fix me*, I thought as I hooked my phone up to the speaker next to the bed to let the sounds of Sabrina Claudio drown out my sorrows. I felt the tracks of my tears rain down my face from the pain I had held in for years of failed relationships. They just rained down my face, draining me of all feelings and hurt in the process and causing anger to take up residence in my heart. *These would be the last tears he got out of me*, I thought as my tears continued to flow. I didn't have a desire to eat, drink, or shower. All I could do was sleep. My pain had drowned out the seconds, the minutes, the hours, and the days. If I hadn't heard banging on my bedroom door, I wouldn't have moved one finger.

"I know you woke! You know what? I'm coming in, and yo' ass better have some clothes on!" I heard Vonka yell as I pulled the covers over my head to block out the light as she pushed the door open and sat on the end of the bed. As I felt her pulling the blanket back, I instantly closed my eyes, because I hadn't had on the light since I had been here. "Now, I let you lay in here and sulk for a week! It's time for you to get your ass out this bed!" Vonka yelled while pulling at the covers that I threw back over myself.

"Ughhhh I know, I know! I just need a couple more hours of sleep," I groaned as I tried to close my eyes back to pretend I was tired, even though I just didn't move because I felt as if I was just swimming in my pain.

"Girl, please, and I'm not going to keep making excuses for you at work! As dancers, our asses are always replaceable! Do you really think that Chris Brown is thirsty for a dancer for his tour? No! So, get yo' butt up because there is money to be made," she announced as she dragged the blanket out of the room behind her, letting me know that when she got back, I had better be showered and ready to go.

I threw my legs over the side of the bed to be able to get ready. After finally dragging myself out of bed to get ready for whatever festivities she had planned, I grabbed my bag to head to the living room to see Vonka at the front door waiting for me with keys in hand.

"How does it feel to be in the land of the living?" she added with a smile as she opened the front door. I followed behind her with a shake of my head. I threw my hands up to cover my eyes as the sun beamed down on me the whole way back to the car.

"Where are you taking me?" I asked, strapping myself in as she continued to make sure her phone was hooked up to Bluetooth as Justin Bieber's "Confident" started playing through the speakers, causing me to snap my neck her way, because I was surprised as hell that she even listened to him with her clatchet ass! Yes, I said clatchet. She was the classiest, but ratchetest woman I had ever met.

"Since when you start listening to Justin Bieber?" I laughed, sitting back in my seat as we headed toward the highway.

"Since his ass started walking around full of tattoos and looking extra fine. That's when, while you all in my business," she added while rapping Chance the Rapper's part.

I knew she had a thing for Chance the Rapper. *That's probably how Vonka knew this damn song*, I thought while shaking my head. Seeing how she didn't tell me to get changed into anything extra fancy, I just knew we weren't going anywhere too exclusive. We pulled into the parking lot of the studio that we had been looking at ever since we'd been on this break from tour. We'd always talked about opening a studio so that we could help women who felt like they had lost their confidence or just in general feel as if they were bold enough to come and dance, learn some choreography, lap dances, twerking classes, and classes for kids. Between Vonka and I, we knew quite a few people that could help teach these classes. We had just been waiting to get the right amount of money saved up to purchase this place.

"Now get yo' ass out," Vonka added while parking the car and hopping out to head toward the front door of the studio.

It was surprisingly open without the "for sale" sign, causing me think that, since I wanted to lay around in my misery, that I had missed out on my dream of having my own studio. I rushed to catch back up Vonka as she stopped at the desk with a stack of papers sitting on the countertop with two glasses and a bottle of the best wine.

"So, I went ahead and made the final down payment on this place! And before I finish, we better get ready to be busier than we have ever been! Plus, I'm trying to be a BBB! So, co-owner, go over there and sign your part, so we can make this money!" she yelled while popping the cork on the wine bottle as I just stood there in pure shock.

"Are you serious? If so, you know I got my part in my savings!" I added, running up to her to hug her.

"You damn right you do. I had to get a temporary loan from Bronx's nasty ass, and we not gon' speak of what this man asked me to do," she added with the most serious expression, like she wasn't happily doing whatever this man asked her to do.

I laughed at my thoughts while signing my name on each dotted line. I was just ready to start my life fresh because that crying and being in love only to have someone not give a damn about anything you feel was for the birds if you asked me.

"Wait, what the hell is BBB?" I asked, giving her a puzzled expression as I watched her step away from the counter and start twerking with her tongue hanging out.

"BBB, that's a bad bitch balling," she said, mimicking exactly how O.T. Genesis said it on the song "Thick".

I swear this girl right was always acting a straight fool. We both looked at each other and were stuck for a minute just to burst out laughing a minute later. This was exactly what friends were for. I didn't know what I would have done without her aggy self.

"We about to show these other shops what we are about in these parts!" I added as we slapped hands. This was exactly what I needed. I had no room for love in my life or drama. It was all about this studio going forward for me.

Later at the park...

Although Vonka had given me the good news that our dreams of finally becoming owners of our own dance studio had finally happened, I still can't get rid of the dreaded feeling, that our dreams would slip through our fingertips at any moment. I talked her into allowing me to have a moment to myself. I needed to let myself feel for a moment. I shouldn't even be out here at this park crying when I just received the news of a lifetime. This was precisely why love wouldn't get a chance to break me again. All that I kept thinking was what was wrong with me? Why was it that none of my relationships lasted? They always ended in drama, which was ridiculous to me. *I deserved better than this,* I thought as I watched all of the cute couples playing with their kids, laughing, and enjoying the life I wished I sometimes had, but it was cool. From this point forward, I was going to be focusing on myself and this business. *I have no room for more tears*, I thought as someone came and sat next to me. I looked up into the face of an older woman who smiled at me as she started to speak softly.

"We've all been there, hun, a time or two in our lives. Life happens to all of us, but it's our job to make lemons into lemonade," she stated as she stood from the bench and left me in my thoughts. I didn't know who she was, but those words reached something in me that let me know I was a fighter and that I wasn't going to lose to love again.

I WAS GLAD ALENA'S ASS HAD FINALLY SNAPPED OUT OF it. Wasn't no piece of dick worth all that bullshit if you asked me. I learned my damn lesson already with that no-good ass nigga Troy, but I was past that. My baby, Bronx, wasn't nothing like that, but I sure wasn't gonna let another nigga get the best of me, and you could believe that. I made my way to the bank to turn in the paperwork that we had signed for the studio that we just couldn't wait to get open. I felt bad that I had to lie to Lena about where I'd gotten this loan from, but I wasn't borrowing from no man so he could tell me what he gave me. I walked inside and made my way toward Mrs. Jefferson. She was the main reason we could pay what we did for this studio. I thought we were never going to be able to start our own studio, but it came right when we needed it. I was headed toward her office when Mrs. Jefferson stepped out to greet me.

"Hey, hun! How have you been?" she asked as I stepped into her office and took a seat.

"I've been pretty good. Just coming in to turn this paperwork in. Alena signed her portion of the contract! We are just ready to get started already!" I smiled.

"Well, you know that son of mine has been asking about you?" she stated with a smile as she took the loan paperwork from me.

I just knew this bullshit was going to happen. I should have just stayed away from this bank, but I was just going to smile and keep my mouth shut because I needed this damn loan.

"I told him I had seen you recently. I would just love to see you guys together again. Don't get me wrong, I know what my son put you through, but I know he has changed. Why don't you just give it one more try?" she asked with a sly smile.

"As much as I would love to do that, Mrs. Jefferson, I have a boyfriend that I'm completely happy with," I added, trying to let her down easy because I had no plans on getting back with Troy's no-good cheating ass. Even if my relationship was a mess, I wouldn't go back.

"Well, hun, you never know. He could be exactly what you need. Hun, I'm doing you a favor right now, and I would hate to be one of those people that has to take my favor away. What would your friend think of you?" She smiled, but I could feel the evil undertones within her voice.

"You know what I could—" I started as she started to shake her head left to right with a smirk on her face.

"I know every loan teller in this state. If you think I won't use that power for you to miraculously not be able to get one, try me. Cut that boy off now, or there will be no dance studio. My son will be giving you a call tonight to set up your date, and if I hear one thing about you turning him down. You will be sorry. Trust me," she added with a smile as she began putting away the loan paperwork.

I just hopped out of my seat and turned on my heels to head out of the office. As I was about to slam the door, I heard her clear her throat. I looked over my shoulder.

"Don't you slam my door, daughter-in-law. See you this Sunday for our family dinner, and you better not be a minute late." She smiled as if we were old friends. I wanted to whoop her ass so bad, but what would that do if Lena and I lost the shop before we even got started? I just knew Bronx wasn't going for none of this.

I drove to clear my thoughts because I couldn't go anywhere with Troy, period. I felt my phone vibrate, and when I got to the light, I took a quick look to see his damn mom worked fast because his no-good ass was already texting me and trying to set up a date. Ugh, could my life get any more hectic? One minute I was on cloud nine. I finally had a man that actually cared about me and my dream studio, but all that came with a price. Should I have picked the man I had been waiting for all my life, or the studio Lena and I have talked about since we were kids? If I chose my man, where would that have left Lena? It was her studio too. I definitely had a lot of thinking to do, that was for sure. I continued to drive down the highway to my secret hideaway.

I finally made my way to the first studio that I had ever danced in. It had become abandoned over the years, but no one ever came here, so when I wanted to let go and just feel in a secure location, I would just come here. I hooked up my Alexa speaker. Good thing I had gotten that wireless base from Amazon because none of the outlets worked in this old building. I would be out here dancing with my thoughts, and I needed to get this horrible ass day out of my mind. I picked up my phone to turn on "I'd Rather Be Alone" by Karyn White. This song always had me in my feelings because it was the story of my life until I met Bronx. Now, here I was with this present issue that it was either he or my shop that I've wanted my whole life. I dropped my bag and turned Alexa up as loud as I could until the sounds of Karyn White echoed against the walls. I stepped in front of the barely there mirror as I tied my hair up when the hook came back around. I still had my heels on, but I didn't give a damn. Dance always healed me. *I won't be a fool, a fool for our love. 'Cause I'd Rather be alone than be here unhappy."* I put every bit of passion into each step I had as I went into a plié and then a relevé as I whipped my body into both directions, causing the ponytail holder that was once in my hair to fall. *"Startin' this time I'm going to think selfishly and never depend on someone else for keepin' me happy, oh, no, no."* I could feel the pain in each word Karyn sang tearing through my body. I ran through jump after jump as the pain of my decision brought me to my knees with tears falling down my face as my hands swept from left to right. I couldn't move anymore because I knew I was going to have to pull away from the greatest love I had experienced to be back in misery at home for my dream. I had fought so long and hard for this. It wasn't just my studio. This was Alena's life savings just as much as it was mine. Who's to say this fairy tale wouldn't come crashing down on top of me anyway. At least I knew the type of bullshit I would be walking into with Troy. I knew he wasn't shit. Bronx had yet to show me that, and I would have rather left on good terms before my vision of him went away. Did I really need to be loved by a man to be happy? No, I didn't. I was going to love me through the misery, because I wasn't going to give love the chance to fuck me over again. This time, I was ending it on my own terms I decided as I cleaned the remaining tracks of tears from my face and began to place everything into my bag so that I could go handle what I had to handle for myself. The minute I stepped outside of the center. Bronx was leaned up against his all-black Rolls Royce with his feet crossed at his ankles, muscles bulging in his gray, black pyramid sweater in all of his light skin glory, beard lined up to perfection, and hair edged up. I looked up as his gray eyes reached mine with his eyebrow raised as he stepped from the car and began to make his way toward me as his long legs ate up the concrete with each purposeful step he took. The minute he reached me, he had yet to say one word to me. I didn't know if he could tell the decision I had come to as he gripped my neck bringing me into the warmth of his body as he tipped my head back to reach my lips. Bronx slowly nipped my bottom lip as I felt his tongue begging for entry. I could never fight the passion he brought every time we were in the same room. The love I felt for him hit me like a freight train as he made love to my mouth with every swipe of tongue, every nip of his teeth, and every feel of his rough hands against my hip as he held on like they were handlebars. I was definitely gonna have to give this shit a little bit more thought than an hour. I might have to kiss the damn studio goodbye, pun intended. As he pulled away, it felt like I was given a drug I could no longer have any more.

"Why you here, Vee?" he asked with the most sincere expression.

"I just had some thoughts to sort out," I responded, looking down at my feet as he gripped my chin to bring my eyes back toward his.

"How you know I was here?" I asked as I pulled away to walk toward my car, because he was looking too intently into my eyes like he was searching for the answers to the world.

"You know the streets talk to me, baby," he stated in a matter of fact tone as I almost snapped my neck to look back over my shoulder to look at him like he had lost his damn mind as a smirk came across his face.

"Don't play with me, Bronx. You told me you were leaving all that shit alone! You are in the pros. What do you need the streets for?" I yelled over my shoulder as I slammed my bag into the back seat of my car and took my heels off to slip on my *Frozen* slippers. I couldn't drive in my sneakers or heels, so my *Frozen* slippers worked wonders.

"Vee, I am. Just because they give me a little info a

time or two doesn't mean anything. Plus, I need to make sure you cool especially since I haven't been able to get in touch with you all day, so don't be out here yelling at me and shit like I'm a child with yo' cute ass slippers on." He smirked, causing a smile to unwillingly come across my face. Bronx is always using jokes to cover up shit he knows he ain't supposed to be doing in the first place. Especially, after hanging with these same dudes almost cost him his place in the NBA, you would think he would learn his lesson.

"Whatever, New York," I stated because I knew he hated it.

"Yeah right," he stated as he began walking up on me as he picked me up off my feet and laid me across my back seat as he tore a hole in the middle of the leggings I had just put on not too long ago.

My nasty ass didn't even stop him. I was stressed out so damn bad. I needed my cookie licked on. I wrapped my legs around his neck as I felt his tongue slip slowly between my lips as his beard began teasing my clit. He leaned up and started sucking on my clit as my essence slid into his mouth. I pulled my body deeper into the back seat as he whipped his dick out to slide it between my lips to get the tip wet. Before I could get it right and wet, he flipped me over onto my knees as he gripped my hair from the back and gripped my neck as he began to punish my pussy from the back. I could feel my essence sliding down my thighs as I screamed out. His mouth latched onto mine, stopping the sound from coming out since I had forgotten entirely we were outside, damn near in the hood, fucking. He let my hair go as I slowly slid off of him and pulled him into the truck to saddle up because I was gonna ride his ass all the way to heaven and back. The minute I got up on top to saddle up, I slowly slid down as I began to make small circles on his tip then sliding down the whole length, causing him to moan out. I latched my teeth onto his bottom lip to show him how it was really done as my ass bounced up and down until I felt his balls began to tighten. I hopped off to slide his pipe down my throat. I tasted the essence of him and I mixed together. There was no taste like it as he spilled everything he had into my mouth. While he gripped my hair, I threw my ass up in the air to feel him stroking each cheek. I made sure to catch every little drop of him in my mouth. I didn't wanna waste one drip. As I cleaned up, I slid my tongue across my bottom lip to make sure none spilled or stayed in my mouth.

"Oh shit! Don't get nothing else started out here in this muthafucka. I'm gonna need you to get your ass to the house, so I can wear that shit out again," he stated as he nipped the corner of my ear while zipping his pants up.

"Man, look what you did to my pants?" he stated, pointing to all the wet spots covering his pipe.

"Looks like you better hurry up and get to the house so I can clean that up for you." I smiled as I fixed my clothes as much as I could and grabbed my mouthwash out of my armrest to rinse my mouth out as he reached over to kiss me in the mouth before rushing to his car so nobody could see the wet spots on his pants.

This decision was going to be way harder than I expected, but I was definitely up to the challenge. I had to find another damn way to get myself out of this shit, but I'd might as well play nice with Troy and his mama until I did.

"ARE YOU READY!?" I YELLED OUT AS I LOOKED OVER at Lavonka, who was still stretching in front of the mirrors as a smile came across her face.

"Been ready, boo. Let's do this thang. Good thing we starting classes with the grown women first. I didn't expect us to pop this quickly," she stated with an excited expression as she hopped off the floor to straighten out her shorts and make sure her heels were still intact.

Since it was our first class, we decided to make it sexy. So why not start our first class with an original piece to "F It Up" by Tank. He had been killing it this year, so we had to start it off with a bang. I walked over to our front desk to make sure the glasses of wine we had out were in order as well as our sign-in sheet as Lavonka walked over to the front door to unlock the door and let everyone know we were open. Our first class was expected to have about thirty girls, so Vonka and I decided to split them up into two groups. She would take one, and I would do the other and teach them the dance. Just watching everyone come in, I was still in disbelief that I had my own studio. I smiled as a group of girls walked in. I walked over to introduce myself, but one of the girls looked familiar, but I just let it go as I invited them in and got them to sign.

"So, ladies, we appreciate y'all being our first group ever to be a part of our studio! So let's have a good time and learn a couple things that we can all bring back home to our fine ass men, side pieces, and bitches! Whatever you got going on, not my business, but it is my business to make sure you look amazing while you're killing this routine!" Vonka yelled out as the girls laughed. I shook my head because this girl was crazy.

I walked up to the front as I looked at everyone. "So, we are splitting y'all into two groups!" I yelled out as everyone made it onto two different sides.

I noticed that the girl who looked familiar to me had decided to stay on my side with her friends. I just shook it off as the sounds of Tank started coming through the speaker. I had everyone spread out to make sure everyone was at an arm's length away from the person next to them. Our studio had a few class-rooms, but we decided to use our biggest one, so we didn't have to be all over the place since we were teaching the same thing. I started off with the first step as Tank sang out. *Rock on it like you a Milly. Yeah, bounce on it like you from Philly. Yeah, so dope how you cut it up.* I strutted in a circle to stop and drop down like I was bouncing on a dick as I dragged my hand from my center up my body and rotated my hips in a circle to come up slowly. Vonka stopped the music, and I looked up to notice everyone in the class was watching me.

"Now, that's how you do that shit!" Vonka yelled as I waved her off. The girl in the back that looked so familiar snickered with her friends while pointing at me.

Vonka looked over at me like she was burning up to say something, but I shook my head no. I didn't need our studio getting a bad rep over something I knew I was good at. *Although I was a thick girl, I could dance my ass off, and you couldn't take that from me,* I thought with a smile as we ignored them and walked around to get everyone through the steps, which, not to my surprise, they were having a hard time grasping the steps. So I walked over to help them when the skinny one with long dark hair looked up at me with a frown. "Bitch, we don't need your help, with your fat ass! I hope you recognize me. We know exactly who you are. I don't know what Quran even see in you," she stated while turning to laugh with her friends.

I drew my arm back to knock her teeth out her mouth when I felt Lavonka push me behind her. "You bitches got to go, unless you down with getting your ass whooped, but we don't do that in our establishment, so make your way out the door," she stated with a smile as they rolled their eyes, knocking stuff over in the process on the way out. The rest of the class watched the scene like all they needed was a bag of popcorn and a chair, and then they would be all set because we undoubtedly almost provided the show. The minute they stepped out the door, Lavonka turned around to look at me with a smirk.

"What is that face for? I am not about to be a part of your crazy schemes," I added with a laugh.

As I turned back around toward the class, who all had been watching the scene. This was exactly what we wanted to avoid was drama in here. We worked too damn hard to have some snot nose bitches in here showing out.

"I'm sorry about all of that. Now, who is ready to finish this? We are not gonna let these girls kill what we were in here doing." As everyone nodded in agreement and got back into place, we decided to finish the class together rather than in groups like we had been doing earlier.

"So, let's take it from the top!" I yelled out as everyone spread out to do the routine all together, and if I do say so myself, besides all of the nonsense that took place earlier, this was a pretty good class. Everyone started to get their things together since our first class was coming to an end.

"So, when is the next class?" one of the women asked, causing everyone to stop and wait for an answer.

"Well, I'm glad you asked! We are also going to start doing some jazz classes for little girls, ballet, tap, contemporary, and hip-hop. So, we will have a couple sign-up sheets up front as well as schedules for different classes. Plus, we can't forget our ladies, so we will definitely be doing more of these classes," I stated in an excited tone as the women nodded their heads and headed out to the lobby.

After everyone left, I locked the doors, turned around, and almost ran right into Lavonka, who had a devious smirk on her face.

"Oh, uh huh, I'm not in the mood for your crazy schemes tonight." I laughed, walking around her as I grabbed a broom out of our utility closet to sweep up the studio with Lavonka right on my heels.

"I don't know what you're talking about, but if you didn't recognize that heffa from earlier, it finally hit me! That's homegirl that was on the date with Quran. You can't tell me you didn't recognize her," she stated quickly while grabbing the cleaning spray to get the mirrors cleaned in the process.

"I knew something was familiar about her, but I couldn't put my finger on it!" I stopped sweeping to look over at Lavonka. I knew she was thinking exactly what I was thinking. "You think that girl knew this was our studio?" I asked as Lavonka looked over at me with her face turned up like she couldn't believe I would even ask her that question.

"Hell yeah, she knew from the second she walked into this bitch," she added as I watched her pick up her phone from behind the counter with a look of disgust on her face.

"I'm going to assume that isn't Bronx, because when he texts you, you look a little bit more like you hopped, skipped, and jumped into heaven," I added as she looked at me with a smirk.

"Whatever, girl, and nope it isn't him... wish it was," she added in a low voice.

I hadn't heard her sound like that since the Troy

situation. Let me find out Bronx was fucking up. "Anyway, I have connections, and you know this. Guess who I have an address to come pop up on?" she added with a big smile as she shook her phone.

"Here you go," I added with a laugh as I went to grab the rest of my things out of our office since we were done for the night.

"What?" she asked as we headed toward the front door to lock it on our way out.

"We are just going to leave the situation alone. I'm not even concerned with Quran anymore. He can stick his little thang wherever he wants to," I added as Vonka smacked her teeth. I turned to lock the studio doors when I heard someone speak.

"You didn't think we were just going to leave after you snuck me that night, bitch!" I looked over at Vonka with a laugh to see she was already pulling her hair up into a bun.

I looked back to notice it was her and just one of her friends. I guess the others decided they didn't want any parts of this situation.

"You just can't take the easy way out and take yo' ass home, huh?" I asked as wiped my hands on my pants to keep from putting my hands on this girl.

I wasn't the violent type unless pushed to take care of a situation, and she definitely had me ready to lay her the fuck out.

"Quran don't want you anymore. Why you think he been calling my phone and taking me on dinners? I guess he came to his senses and realized you're not anything but a fat bitch who thinks she can dance," she added with a laugh as she looked over at her friend who laughed right along with her.

I was getting really tired of having to defend something that didn't bother me not one damn bit. I nodded my head as I started to head to my car without another word. This girl was just purely miserable, because if he were her man, she wouldn't be worried about what I was doing but about what he was doing.

"Well, as much as we all would love to sit out here and enjoy your analysis of my weight and dance skills, I have to be here tomorrow morning to open my studio. So, you young ladies have a good night. I'm sure your man is waiting for you at home, right," I added with a smile as her snickers stopped instantly, because I wasn't entertaining her like she expected.

I looked over at Vonka, who was feening for a good fight. She looked at me like I had grown another head but threw her hands up and started heading to her car.

"This isn't finished!" homegirl yelled as I waved goodbye while getting in the passenger side of Vonka's car.

I knew she was pissed, because she hated to walk away from a fight, but I really just didn't care. We finally made our dreams happen, and I wasn't going to celebrate our first night of having class by fighting some washed-up hoe who wanted my leftovers. No, that just wasn't going to happen. I looked over at Lavonka, since we had been sitting in silence for a good thirty minutes, and usually, she was a ball of energy.

"So, what was all of that about back there?" she asked smoothly.

"I'm not rewarding these hoes with any more of my energy. I'm just not in the business of fighting over a man that I'm not even remotely concerned about anymore. Good luck to her on that one," I added as I gazed out the window because that was all I had to say on the subject.

"Normally, I would have something to say back to that shit, but I guess you're right. I just needed to let some steam off, and yo' ass made us leave a good fight," she added with a laugh.

I shook my head at her, because I knew she was as serious as a heart attack.

"Well, our grown asses shouldn't be fighting anyway. We made it, sis! We have talked about this damn shop since we were about six years old. I'm not losing it for anybody, and I know you feel the same way I do!" I added as she nodded her head almost like she was in deep thought about something.

"I just think there is a bigger goal than that now. Plus, I think we should get involved with a mentor program for young girls. We used to wish we could have that kind of influence to look up to when we were younger," I added as I looked over to see she was still in her own world.

"Vonka!" I yelled to get her attention.

"What? Girl, I heard you. I was just thinking, and I don't think that's a bad idea at all," she added as we pulled up to the front of her house.

She went to undo her seat belt as I gripped her wrist. "Hey, are you alright? You've been spaced out a lot lately," I asked as she put a smile on her face shaking her head, while still removing her seat belt at the same time.

"I'm good, but it takes a little time to believe that your life is going as good as it is, don't you think?" she asked as I nodded my head because I just walked out of hell and was making my way back to heaven as we spoke.

I just needed to leave the male species alone, because they didn't ever do me any good. "I guess you're right," I stated as we headed toward the front door.

"I know I'm right. When have I ever steered you wrong?" she asked with a smile on her face.

"Multiple times. I know you remember that time in high school when—" I started as she interrupted me.

"Well, as of recent, and why you always bringing up old stuff?" she added as she walked in ahead of me.

"It not my fault that you always think you have the best plans, and they fall through," I added with a laugh.

"So, where you think you going looking like that?" I heard over my shoulder as I looked over to see Bronx leaned against the wall in all his fine ass glory with a smirk coming across his face. I watched him eye my ass as I bent over and tried to find my damn shoes that just wouldn't pop up.

"While you over there just eying my ass, can you help me find my damn shoes? I can't find them anywhere!" I yelled as I ran my hand through my hair to look back over at him. As he held back his smile, he stepped away from the wall and moved around me to reach the top shelf, pulling down my box of shoes I had spent the last forty-five minutes trying to find.

"Thanks," I responded as I walked back into the room to have a seat at the end of my bed. I watched him squat down in front of me as Bronx removed each shoe from the box and went to reach for my foot.

"What are you up to?" I asked with a soft smile.

"I can't take care of my baby?" he asked with a smirk as he placed each foot into my shoes.

"So, where you going looking like this?" he asked as I hopped up to grab my bag from the side table.

"I have a business meeting for the loan, babe," I added as I started out the room when I felt him grip my wrist to pull me back.

"Uh huh, bring that ass back here. We still doing dinner tonight? You know I'm getting ready to be out of town with the team for a few weeks, remember?" he asked while wrapping his arms around my waist and pulling me against his chest.

"Mmmhmm, we still having dinner. Don't think I'm playing about you video chatting me every night. If I even think you got a bitch with you—" I started as he leaned in to suck my bottom lip into his mouth. I instantly wrapped my arms around his neck, bringing him closer as I slipped my tongue into his mouth. I immediately felt his hands gripping my ass as I pushed his chest with him laughing in the process.

"Mmmhmm, I heard you. Gone take care of yo' business, baby. Make sure yo' ass back in time, or I'm eating without you!" he added as he slapped my ass while walking around me to head back into the bathroom.

"Whatever, boy!" I added as I walked out to rush to my car because this old devil ass bitch was working on my damn nerves. I still couldn't believe I had gotten myself into this bullshit ass situation, but there wasn't much I could do now but deal until I found a way out.

My ringtone started sounding throughout the car, alerting me to the fact that this fuck boy was calling me.

"Yes?" I answered as I rolled my eyes.

"Wassup, baby. I'm trying to figure out how you're getting to lunch. You know my mom ain't gonna be feeling you being late or showing up not on my arm," he added in a voice filled with sugar.

"Number one, stop calling me baby. We both know I'm only dealing with this shit for the time being, and you know as much as I do what the fuck you did that jacked-up our relationship, so test me if you want to! I will air all of your shit out!" I yelled as I heard him take a deep breath in.

"Yeah, man, I know, but you know I'm right, and how the fuck you think my mom is going to act when she finds out you haven't let that nigga go?" he added in a bright tone. He just made me so sick.

"Meet me at the Walmart at the restaurant, but after this bullshit ass lunch, you are taking me right back to my car!" I yelled. I was just exhausted with the whole situation, and I hadn't even made it to the real nonsense yet.

"I got this," he added as I hung up in his face because I definitely felt like he was enjoying this situation a tad bit too much.

Walmart Parking Lot

This man really had me fucked up, I thought as I hopped out of my Mercedes Benz that Bronx had bought me for my birthday. I knew it was fucked up, right? Driving the shit my boyfriend bought me to go have lunch with my ex and his damn mama. I rolled my eyes to see him standing outside his car with a bouquet of red roses with the cheesiest grin coming across his face. I put my car in park as I pulled my visor down to look at my appearance one more time to make sure not a hair was out of place. I let myself out the car, locking my doors in the process, and walked right past him going straight to the passenger door. I saw his smile fall while watching him try to rush to my door to open it for me.

"I got it," I snapped as I opened the door for myself to have a seat.

This situation just felt like bullshit to me. *There just had to be another way out of all of this*, I thought to myself not realizing he had gotten into the driver side and pulled back into traffic. I finally looked over at him to see he had thrown the flowers in the back seat, so I snatched them up and brought them up to my nose when I noticed him smiling out the corner of my eye.

"Do you like them?" he asked in a hopeful tone as I started rolling the window down to answer his question.

I threw the whole bouquet out the window. I watched Troy's eyes become the size of saucers while looking around like a bitch to see if there were any cops in the area.

"What the fuck, Vonka?" he asked with an attitude.

I didn't feel the need to play nice with a mutha-fucka that couldn't stand up to his mom that was willing to ruin my life to keep his life in balance. Just thinking about it made me want to tell him to pull this damn car over, so I could whoop his ass like the bitch he was being. I stayed silent because I knew, if he said some slick shit to me, I was knocking the taste out of his mouth before we even made it to the damn lunch. We wouldn't be able to explain the black eye her son was going to be sporting, which was going to put my business in jeopardy, and he wasn't worth it.

"When we get to this damn restaurant, you go with whatever I say," I stated as we pulled up to the front of the restaurant and valet walked up to open my door. I looked back over at him to make sure he heard precisely what I said. He nodded his head in response. I didn't know how I was ever attracted to him. *Now that I had a real one, there was no way I could go back*, I thought as he went to grab my hand. I almost elbowed him in his stomach on reflex alone as I held it together until we made it to the table with his mother, who was smiling like today was the best day of her life while I was dying inside with each second that passed with them in my presence. I watched Mrs. Jefferson gracefully remove herself from her chair to come hug and kiss both of our cheeks when she whispered in my ear.

"Oh, honey, you better perk up if you want to keep that little studio," she added with a devious smile as she walked around to her side of the table. I just wanted to snatch her wig right the hell off at this moment, but I just relaxed and began to think of Bronx to make me get comfortable.

"So, how has the reconnecting been going?" she asked after they brought around our drinks.

"It's been going as well as to be expected with it being a forced situation and all," I added with a smirk. I looked over to see that Troy's eyes had gotten big. He was not expecting me to say that, but I was sick of playing nice already.

"Oh, is that right?" she added as she looked over at her son who kept trying not to meet her eyes.

"Son, speak up for yourself. How is everything going? Can I be expecting a wedding soon?" she asked as he smiled and nodded his head while both of their eyes looked back toward me with expectant expressions.

"Oh, is that right, Lavonka? I just love the fact that, once you're married, this studio loan will be final, don't you?" she added while trying to grip my hand.

"Oh, so this was your game plan all along?" I laughed as the smile fell from her face. "Well, you can forget that shit right now! I won't be marrying into shit! You and your son can go straight to hell!" I yelled as I abruptly pushed my chair back and made my way outside as the valet brought around Troy's Car. Without a second thought, I took the keys, and I took off, leaving him and his punk ass mama at this restaurant. I drove back to the Walmart parking lot, put his keys under the mat in his car, and whipped out of the lot to head back home because I needed to be in my man's presence after this bullshit. When I felt my phone buzz, I looked down to see a text had come in.

Mrs. Jefferson: *You just made the biggest mistake of your career. Kiss that studio goodbye! You will be back!*

I threw my phone in the back seat as I made my way back home, driving as fast as I could. I walked through the front door to hear the TV playing in the living room. I made a beeline toward the sounds of the TV.

"Baby, where are you?" I asked.

"I'm in the living room. How did the meet—" he started as I threw myself into his lap and began kissing him like he was the last breath I needed to survive.

I felt his hand began to slide down my back to caress my hips as he gripped my ass while lifting me up from the couch as I wrapped my legs around his waist. I began to drag my lips down his neck as he made his way toward our bedroom. He let me out of his arms as he set me back on my feet to slowly peel every piece of clothes from my body as he threw each article of clothing from my body. I trembled as he kissed each soft spot on my body that made me tingle with excitement. When he got to my red lace thongs, I pushed his head back as I began to walk back toward my bed with a soft smile coming across my face and laid back on the bed.

"You're just so beautiful. I want you to know that," he stated as he dragged my thongs down my thighs as he leaned down to caress my legs.

He rained kisses down my thighs, and he began to French kiss my lips while dipping his tongue in between to catch everything I was giving. As he stepped back to remove all of his clothes, I couldn't do anything but stare. He was just so beautiful. It was hard as hell not to. A smirk started to come across my face as I bit my lip and spread my legs wide as I began to dip my fingers in and out of my pussy as I started to moan out. I watched him step toward me and stop as I slid my soaking wet fingers into my mouth to clean all of my juices off my fingertips. Without hesitation, he came in between my legs throwing each leg over his shoulder as he leaned in to tongue me up nastily while I began to feel pressure from his thick tip begging for entry.

"Mmm, daddy like that," I moaned out as he began to take long deep strokes until he started to knock it out the frame.

He dropped one of my legs so he could get deep as I cried out with each stroke he gave. He flipped me over onto my stomach as he pulled me onto my knees. I automatically began to throw it back as my ass clapped while he continued to stroke me.

"Haaarderr," I moaned out as he gave it to me just how I begged for it.

"I'm about to cum!" I moaned as I spilled all over his pipe.

"Ughh," he moaned out as he emptied himself into me as we both hit the mattress out of breath.

I slid under his arm to get closer to him as he hopped up to grab a rag. He began washing me down between my legs and wiping his pipe down.

"So what's been going on, baby?" he asked as he laid back next to me to cuddle up.

"Just stress, that's all. Enough about me, you looked

a little wore out today. By the way, where is Lena? I didn't see her car outside," I asked as I looked over to see him take a deep breath, so I knew some stupid shit had to have happened while I was gone.

"Man, she out with Nash. She's good. I'll tell you about that shit later," he added as he began nibbling on my neck.

"Stop playing." I laughed, trying to figure out how did he persuade Lena to take even one step toward him. She had sworn off men since the Quran situation.

"I'm being real they out somewhere, but I want to know what's really up with you. Not that stress shit you throwin' at me. I know it's more than that, I've been with you long enough to know the difference," He responded while turning me around to face him.

"Sometimes, I just feel like this is all too good to be true ya' know. It's like I know you're real because I feel the way you make me feel any time you step in the room with me. But at the same time, you make me feel things I didn't think existed after everything I've been through," I replied as he moved a loose strand from my face and behind my ear.

"I don't think you realize how special you are, I'm the one receiving a gift baby not the other way around. You know better than anybody some of the shit I've been through with my parents. I've never witnessed a love like this, the streets raised me but I made it out with basketball. You're my saving grace baby, next to basketball without you I would have never experienced real love," He stated as he leaned down to caress my lips with his.

"That was sweet baby, but I'm still trying to figure out how you persuaded Lena to go on a date," I added trying to change the subject. I looked up at him watching as he leaned down, and begun sliding his tongue over my nipples.

"YOU NEED to be trying to be trying to figure out how to get yo' man dick back soft," he added as he pressed his pipe into my center. I moaned out while wrapping my arms around his neck.

I guess the problems of today were going to have to wait until tomorrow because my man definitely needed all my attention right now.

Earlier that Day

I COULDN'T BELIEVE AFTER ALL OF THOSE TOURS AND dancing to get gig after gig that I was a co-owner of my own dance studio. *This was all Vonka and I talked about when we were kids,* I thought as I rolled around to burrow deeper into the crisp sheets of my bed. I needed to get back on my feet and find my own place, since I was crashing with Vonka and Bronx at the moment. Ever since that lame ass boy tried to play me, I would never understand why in the hell he continued to call me. Probably was calling me because his little side bitch and the Muppets, showed up and showed out at the studio. Vonka and I almost had to tag they asses but it wasn't even worth it. I was getting tired of these scheming hoes taking my kindness for weakness, because I wasn't the one you wanted to fuck with. I couldn't stand hating ass bitches who couldn't stand to see another woman doing something for themselves.

Shoot, if you asked me, she should be happy I didn't continue to whoop her ass that night I caught her out with Quran's no-good ass. I threw the covers from my body as I headed to my dresser to find the perfect outfit to wear for some apartment shopping. Who doesn't like going to apartments and taking tours? Plus, although I loved staying with my girl, all she did was fuck and sleep. I laughed as I finished getting myself together.

I walked out into the living room to see Bronx watching the game with one of the finest men I had seen in a long time. *But right now, I'm on a no men diet, so his beautiful chocolate Morris Chestnut looking ass was going to have to move on out the way, because I am not getting caught up in all of that*, I thought as I checked out his side profile.

"Hey, Bronx, when Vonka gets back, if she asks for me, tell her I'm out apartment shopping," I stated as I made my way past them to head into the kitchen.

"Aight. I got you," he added as he looked at me briefly and then back toward the TV.

But his friend was acting like I was the last supper as I watched him hop up from the couch as I made my way around the island toward the door.

"Yo, wait up, ma. I'll introduce myself since this rude ass man didn't," he added while reaching his hand out and looking over his shoulder, laughing.

Boy, if I didn't think this man was fine before, his ass brought his looks up a whole ten notches more, because he had the perfect set of pearly white teeth with the most bomb smile, causing me to instantly become wet.

"Whatever, with yo' black ass!" I heard Bronx yell from the living room.

I laughed, throwing my hand up to cover the smile coming to my face.

"This man ain't that funny, but I'm Nashoba, but everyone calls me Nash," he stated with a smirk as he looked down at his hand that I had yet to acknowledge, so I placed my hand into his. This man was extremely too fine, and this was the kind of man that had bitches lined up around the corner. If he was hanging with Bronx, I was sure he was in the league, which I didn't want any parts of.

If Quran's regular broke ass would cheat, what am I going to do with a man who can get some from any girl he meets? You could count me out.

"And your name?" he asked again. I didn't realize I had spaced out like that.

"Uh, sorry. Alena, but everyone calls me Lena. Nice to meet you," I responded as I finally pulled my hand out of his to head toward the door, because I needed to get as far as possible from this man. He already had me losing my mind, and all I had was a damn name and a smile.

"Aye, why don't you just go with her to keep her company. I'm sure she would enjoy that," I heard Bronx state as I almost broke my neck to look his way as he burst out laughing.

"No, I'm good by myself," I stated with a quickness as I pulled the door open to head out while bumping right into the one person I had been trying to forget all about.

"Hey, how you been?" he asked with a soft smile coming across his face.

"I've been just fine, Quran. What the hell do you want?" I asked as I crossed my arms across my chest.

"Baby, I'm just trying to work all of this out. Everything wasn't what it seemed," he added.

"Oh, it was exactly what it seemed like. You're a lame ass nigga. I'm going to need you to find a stupid bitch because I'm not the one," I stated in a calm tone as I watched the smile he had on his face fall.

He instantly went and gripped his hands around my neck. I started smacking him in the face so that he would remove his hands.

"Bitch, I don't know who you think you're talking to, but regardless of what you're talking about, you're gon' be my girl or nobody's," he stated with finality as I instantly felt hands pulling us apart.

I looked up to notice it was Bronx while his friend Nash started whopping Quran's ass. I thought this would be a blow for blow fight with how much he used to manhandle me. It had gotten so bad that Bronx let me go as he smoothly walked over to break up the fight.

"Get yo' bum ass out my yard and don't come back, or we gon' have ourselves a problem," I heard Bronx state in nothing over an inside voice.

Quran looked up like he wanted a problem as Nash yelled, "Bring yo' ass back around here if you want!" Bronx looked back over at me to check and make sure I was all right. Bronx reached into his pants, pulling his Glock out and putting it to Quran's temple because his ass wasn't moving fast enough.

"Now, I'm only gon' tell you this shit one more time. I'm starting to think yo' ass should have been on the little bus. Now, you know about me, so you know you received a blessing from God, right? Now I don't repeat myself. The next time I tell yo' ass to raise up out my yard, and you don't make that shit haste, you gon' be leaving aight, but you gon' be in a body bag. You got that?" he stated in a smooth tone as I watched Quran nod his head quickly.

Bronx pulled the gun away from his temple, and Quran hopped up so damn fast to get to his car, he tripped over his own damn feet to get gone.

He looked over his shoulder one last time at me as he yelled out the window of his car. "I'm gon' see yo' ass again, bitch!" His tires screeched going around the corner at top speed.

Bronx waited until he couldn't see his car anymore as he put his strap back up and smoothly walked up the steps while stopping at the door to look over his shoulder with a smooth smile like his crazy ass didn't just go mad psycho killer five seconds ago.

"Aye, I was joking earlier about you riding with her, but after that bullshit, Vonka would kill me if you don't ride with her," he stated as I went to interrupt him.

"You don't have to do that. He is harmless," I added as they both turned to look at me like I had lost my mind.

"I'm not sure if you saw the same nigga we just saw, but I don't give a damn. Which car we taking? Yours or mine?" he asked while pulling his keys out his pocket already heading toward his car.

I guess he answered the question for me, I thought as he walked around to the passenger door to open it for me.

"Come on," he stated as I put a little pep in my step to get into the passenger seat.

Nash

I didn't know what this girl had going on. How did I go from meeting her to doing anything to make sure she was safe? This feeling was foreign to me. I didn't need these kinds of problems. Not only was I in the league, but getting caught up in shit like this could get me into a lot of nonsense that I was just not ready for.

"Did you hear me?" I heard her ask as I glanced over in her direction.

"I said, do you even know where you're going? We have passed the apartment complex two times," she stated with an attitude.

"Aye, do you want to be catching an Uber? Because the last time I checked, I wasn't the one getting choked the hell out, so sit back and relax in this muthafucka. Damn!" I added as I glanced over her way to see she was pissed, but I didn't give a damn.

I pulled into the parking space at the front office as I turned in my seat to give her childish ass a pep talk like she was a child because she was not about to get out this car and show out with me.

"When we get out this car, you are going to act like an adult, correct?" I asked as she looked over at me without expression at all.

"Yeah," she responded as I hopped out the car and ran around to her side to open the door for her.

She stepped out and went right past me without a

thank you in sight, but the view was hella beautiful, if I did say so myself. *Lord give me strength with this one*, I noted and said a silent prayer to myself.

We had been to about four or five different complexes. I couldn't even keep count anymore. I was glad she finally dropped that attitude she had earlier. Lena ended up finding a quaint studio apartment. I couldn't understand the purpose of getting a studio apartment, especially with the budget she was going for. She could have afforded something bigger. But I guess location was a significant factor in her decision making too, since the studio was right down the street from it.

"Hungry?" I asked as I watched her try to cover up the smile that I saw causing her dimples to peek through.

"Starving," she added.

"What do you have a taste for?" I asked as I continued to just drive around until we figured out exactly what we wanted to eat.

"Yeah, how about some Wynwood Kitchen & Bar," she added as I nodded, not surprised by her choice at all.

"You got it," I responded as I leaned down to turn the radio up as the sounds of "Saved" by Khalid started playing. I instantly began to nod my head as I glanced over at her to notice she was staring at me with a surprised expression.

"What? You don't know about Khalid? Homie is dope," I stated as I belted out, "*So I'll keep your number. 'Cause I hope one day I'll get the pride to call you to tell you that no one else is gonna hold you down the way I do."* I ran my free hand down her curls as she laughed at my antics.

"Maybe you should just stick to playing ball." She started laughing as I shook my head as I finally found a park.

"People just ungrateful these days." I laughed as I got out to open the passenger door for her.

"I'm just trying to make sure you didn't have any dreams of being a singer after your ball days were done," she added smartly over her shoulder as I held the door of the restaurant open for her.

Once we were seated at a table and we both ordered our meals, I leaned back in my seat and just admired the beauty that was before me. I just couldn't help to zero in on her plump lips with eyes low showing off what I was sure was her Asian descent along with jet black curly hair that surpassed her shoulders. To make matters better, she was thick in all the right places. I'd always liked my women with a little bit more meat on the bone than others.

"Are you done?" she asked, pulling me out of my thoughts as I nodded my head with a smirk coming across my features.

"I'm just admiring how beautiful you are," I responded in a matter of fact tone.

"Well, thank you, and I wanted to apologize for how we met. Also, how I acted earlier. I'm just not used to anyone doing anything for me without wanting something in return," she stated with a small smile while throwing her mass of jet-black hair over her shoulder.

"It's cool. I just want to get to know you a little better besides what I saw earlier," I asked as I leaned back in my seat.

"Well, if you don't already know, I love to dance, and now that Vonka and I have this studio, our dreams have been fulfilled. We talked about opening a studio since we were like six years old. Now, look at us. We finally have it. Well, enough of that, I'm an only child. My parents and I are pretty close, but they live in North Carolina now since they retired. So Vonka is the only family I have here," she stated as our dishes were placed in front of us.

"So I'm assuming from homie who came up earlier that you're single," I asked as I began to cut up my steak and waited for a response.

"Yeah, you assumed right, and I don't have any intentions of getting caught up like that again." I looked up to see she was focused on her plate almost like she was in a deep thought.

"That supposed to mean anything to me? Because I find you quite interesting and beautiful." I smirked as I watched her look up at me like I had lost my mind while I continued eating my steak.

"Yeah, it usually means don't try, because I'm not interested," she added with an attitude while setting her fork down.

"Hmm, so you say. Although your mouth is telling me you're not interested, your eyes are telling me a whole different story," I stated while setting my fork down as well to lean back in my seat.

"You're so full of yourself. Since you're so smart,

what are my eyes telling you?" she asked as she picked her fork back up to keep her hands busy I'm sure.

"Well, first, I'm not full of myself, just confident in something I know to be true. Second, your eyes are telling me you're interested in where this can go, but because of your last failed relationship, you don't even want to stick your hand back into that cookie jar. Almost like you have some war going on internally with cupid. Does that sound about right?" I asked as she threw her hand up, trying to get our waiter over to the table. I laughed to myself because this woman was off her shit, but it was cool. I liked a little crazy. That meant you loved a little harder than most.

"Can we get the check and a box?" she asked as the waiter nodded and walked off to get everything as she looked back over at me with a scowl on her face.

"As soon as he gets back, I need you to take me home," she stated as she averted her eyes to anywhere but me. Maybe I pushed her too hard too soon.

"My bad if I offended you—" I started before she cut my spill short instantly, letting me know she wasn't trying to hear anything I had to say.

"You think you know so much, but it wasn't just one failed relationship. It was one of many, and I have no intentions of letting love come in and get to me again. So, if that's what you're looking to give me, keep that shit. Now, sex I just might give you, but I don't want the rest," she added in a serious tone as she crossed her arms across her chest.

Before I could get a word out, the waiter was coming to

our table and was boxing up our food as I paid for the meal and left a tip. We stepped out into the fresh air and headed toward my car when she abruptly stopped in the middle of the parking lot. I turned to see if she had dropped something, but she just was standing there looking crazy as hell,

"You drop something?" I asked as I started heading her way when she threw her hand up in a motion to stop me.

"No, umm, I'm going to just take an Uber, okay?" she stated in an unsure tone. I don't know if she had lost her damn mind or what, but I had no intentions of leaving her here.

"Aye, stop playing around. You aren't taking no damn Uber. If you don't want to fuck with me, cool. I got that shit back at the table when you asked for the check. Now come get your ass in this car. Damn!" I yelled as I turned back around to head over to the passenger side to see she had put a pep in her step to get in the car.

It was ridiculous that you have to talk to a woman like that to get her ass to think straight, I thought as I slammed her door shut to get back in on my side. The whole damn car ride was silent, and after the day I had with her crazy ass, I was definitely rethinking trying to break these damn walls down. Especially if this is how she was acting, and I hadn't even put this dick in her life yet. Shit, once that happened, her ass might have been trying to cut me or something if she even thought I was fucking up.

"Hey, umm, I just wanted to apologize for driving

you crazy today. Can we just call it friends?" she asked with a small smile.

This is precisely what I was talking about, I thought as I shook my head with a smirk. I pulled back up in front of Bronx's house. I was just not going to dignify that shit with a response because I had no intentions of being her friend, so she could take that shit and throw it right out the window. I got out to open the door for her, and the minute her feet touched the walkway, I took her hand and pulled her into my chest.

"Yeah, we cool," I added as I gripped her chin to tip up toward me as I slid my tongue across the slit of her lips with her automatically opening up to me.

She was a little stiff a first until she wasn't. When she threw her arms around my shoulders, I slid my hand down her back to get a good grip of all that ass she had. I pulled back to give her some air because I would have happily died to keep the feeling of her plump, soft lips against mine. Once she realized what had happened, she started walking toward the door with significant strides.

"Have a good night," I added with a laugh as I shook my head and headed toward my car, pulling off once I saw she was in the house.

This woman was definitely going to shake up my life, but I was looking forward to it.

Lavonka

"MA'AM WE CANNOT ACCEPT YOUR APPLICATION FOR A business loan today, I apologize." This was the same shit I kept hearing since that bogus ass lunch last week.

I had been trying to find another bank that would give us the loan, but this old bitch had gotten to everybody, so now, no one wanted to work with me not one bit.

"Well, thanks for nothing," I stated sweetly as I picked up my binder filled with my business plan.

I started making my way to my car, and the closer I got, it pissed me off more because Troy was leaned against my car like it was his shit. Every time I saw his ass, it made me want to reshoot his ass.

"Get the hell off my car," I stated as I walked around to my back seat to put my binder and purse back there.

"Why you always so damn hostile?" he asked as I gave him a disgusted look because he knew exactly why I was so damn hostile.

"Don't fuck with me today, Troy! You and your trifling ass mama need to stop fucking with my life!" I yelled as other people in the parking lot all looked over at me like I was crazy.

This was precisely why I couldn't be around him. He always had me ready to go straight to fucking jail.

"I have nothing to do with it! Nobody told you to go to her bank for a loan. You got yourself put back on her radar; not me!" he yelled back as he looked around to see if those same people who were staring at me were outside with us still staring.

"Oh, please! She probably had already been checking for me! And this shit still doesn't change the fact that you know what's up! You need to let your damn mother know what you really want because I have nothing to offer you," I stated as I pushed him to the side to get into my car.

Before I could slam the door shut, he gripped the door to keep it from closing.

"You know I can't do that! And neither will you! Why can't you just act right? My mother sent me to let you know that she forgives your little outburst, and that if you start back making your weekly lunches with her and dates with me, she won't pull your funding," he stated in a desperate voice.

"Fuck you and your mother! When you get the balls to tell her pussy isn't your favorite taste on the menu, then give me a call!" I yelled as he stepped away from the car with a shocked expression.

I slammed my door and made my way to the studio because I definitely had some thinking to do, but it was going to have to wait since today was our first set of classes for the teenagers and kids.

I pulled up to the studio to see Lena at the door holding a sheet of paper at the door with a confused expression.

"What are they talking about?" she asked as she handed me the paper from the bank saying that if we didn't receive the proper funding, we would have to give the studio back to go back out on the market.

We only had sixty days to figure everything out. This was the moment I had been dreading since I first had gotten caught up with Troy and his damn mother.

"It's a really long story, Lena, but I'm trying to fix it," I stated in a tired voice as I unlocked the door of the studio to go inside with her right on my heels.

I knew she was not going to just sweep the issue under the rug just because I didn't want to talk about it anymore.

"What do you mean you're trying to fix it? You do realize this is both of our savings in this right?" she asked as I turned around.

"I realize that more than you know! If you want the real, cool, I'll to give it to you!" I yelled as she crossed her arms over her chest waiting for my response.

"I went out looking for us a new loan because the loan I had gotten approved for was through Troy's mother. I didn't find out it came with strings attached until I went to sign the final paperwork. Do you know her old ass started blackmailing me to date her son? Next thing I know, I'm going on dates and lunches with them just to keep this place going! Until the minute her ass planned my marriage and told me that if I didn't marry her son within the next month all bets were off," I stated.

"Why didn't you tell me this? You said you got the funding from Bronx," Lena asked.

"What would you have done? And I know. I didn't know want you worried about that after all you were going through."

"You're right there, but I could have offered a little support. Shit, we could have come up with other ideas. Did you ever ask Bronx for the loan? I know he would have given it to you," she asked as I started putting my things away so that we could stretch.

"Not really, he's offered, but this has been our dream since we were little, and I don't want anyone saying they gave me my dream, which is why I have been looking at other banks for a loan, but this bitch has connections with all of them! So I have been getting denied left and right, which is why I have on this damn suit!" I stated as I went into our locker room to change.

"Well, damn, this is definitely a sticky ass situation," she stated as she hung up her coat next to me as I changed.

"You ain't gotta tell me that! I have to figure something out, but I don't want to talk about this stressful shit anymore before this class. I need to be stress free before I teach."

"Alright, if I figure out a solution, I'll let you know. We don't have much time to get twenty thousand dollars, but see ya out there," she stated as she walked ahead of me, leaving me in my thoughts.

If I was going to give these kids the time of their lives today, this studio drama had to stay in here. Stressing about the future is pointless right now. I was still living my dream now, even if it felt like it would be just for a moment. The minute I walked out into the studio, Lena had music playing as she stretched in front of the mirror because we would be open in the next twenty minutes.

We had finally made it through the classes. To think, I thought the adults would tire me out, but the kids? Lawwwd that was another story, but this was exactly what Lena and I dreamed of as little girls. *So, there was no way I was letting my dream slip between fingertips,* I thought as I walked the last set of parents out the door to see a black Taurus driving by slowly. I didn't know who that was, but it better not be those bucket head bitches that came here wanting a problem with Lena. I locked the front door behind me as I made my way back into the studio to see Lena sweeping out the studio.

"So, how you think that went?" I asked with a big grin on my face.

"Amazing, did you see the little one with the cute puff balls that kept falling, but she would hop right back up and try again. She reminds me so much of us when we were her size," she responded with a big smile coming across her face.

"You're talking about Khia? Yeah, she was the cutest. I think they might have been more fun to teach than the grownups." I laughed as she nodded her head in agreement.

"I can agree with you on that! Oh yeah, with all the craziness going on, I didn't get a chance to tell you I got the place! I'm moving in tomorrow, so you and yo' man can continue to screw all over the house without me being there," she announced.

I walked up to her to envelop her in a hug.

"I'm happy for you, girl. You are doing the thang, and we were doing that while you were there, so I didn't miss out on nothing," I added with a smirk.

"Yo' ass is so nasty, so what you going to do about the loan?" she asked as I rolled my eyes. I was hoping she had forgotten, but I should have known better than that shit. She couldn't help herself but to be a pain.

"To be honest, I don't even know what the hell I'm going to do. I'm probably going to have to make a trip and kiss this bitch's ass for the time being until I find another way out," I stated as I took a deep breath in, taking in the realization that I was going to have to put on a show just to keep this shop.

"There has got to be another way! Does Bronx know about this shit?" she asked as we walked over to the mirror to have a seat on the ground.

"Well, when you find it, let me know because I have been to almost every bank in the area to get this damn loan approved, and hell no, he doesn't know. I don't need my man going back to his old ways because he would kill Troy if he found out. Plus, he is going to be pissed because I was supposed to break up with him, but I just can't do it, Lena. I tried when she first started blackmailing me. But I can't, and I can't just let go of our dream either," I stated in a somber tone as a lone tear slid down my cheek.

I was getting sick of all of this. Why did love have to be so fucking hard? It was almost like I was supposed to be alone. I just didn't want to believe that, because I knew that Bronx was made for me. This wasn't just something temporary. I had yet to meet a man that loved me the way he did.

"Hey, we are going to fix this. I hate to agree with you, but until we do, you may have to agree to this bull-shit ass relationship," she stated, wiping the tears from her face.

"Yeah, I know I'll call and let her know the good news in the morning I guess, but I'm surely not doing that shit today. I saw Troy earlier and cursed his ass clean out. I need him to flourish in that shit. Maybe he will think about what I said and get us out this fucked-up situation. That's the least he could do," I stated as I hopped up to head to the locker room to get the rest of my shit.

"Yeah, we know that shit ain't happening. Troy is one of the most selfish people we have ever met," she stated as I laughed because I knew that better than anybody. I thought back to that day that signified the end of our relationship and a trip to the hospital for him.

A year earlier...

"Girl, let me take my ass home. I want to surprise my man, since we got home sooner than we thought," I stated as I grabbed my bag from underneath the tour bus.

"*Oh well, don't let me hold you up. You know Quran's big head ass will be blowing my phone up soon, and I don't need to hear his mouth.*" *She laughed as she hugged me while heading to her car.*

This tour was one of the most extended tours I had been on, and I just couldn't wait to lay up under my man and get a bomb ass massage. I knew he missed me. It had been a couple weeks since I had been home. I pulled up to my house to notice that his car was in the driveway. Too bad for surprising him. I figured he would be at work. I unlocked the door, and as I placed my bags by the door, I saw there were two wine glasses on the table. I know this muthafucka ain't in here drinking my damn wine with some other bitch. *I leaned down into my purse to pull out my gun as I cocked it, because he had me entirely fucked up. I started to creep up the steps, making my way toward our room, when I heard groaning the closer I got to our door.* I'm getting ready to kill this muthafucka. *Before I could push the door open, I heard him moan out.* "*Oh, shit, Erick suck that shit.*"

I stopped mid push as I stepped away from the door to try and replay back what I had just heard. Not only was this mutha-fucka in my room fucking somebody that ain't me, but now he fucking men! Oh hell nah! I pushed the door open to a sight that almost made me throw up in my damn mouth. Erick was down on his knees with a mouthful of Troy's dick. I just wanted to shoot that shit right off into his mouth as he turned around with a shocked expression while pushing Erick away from him.

"*Nah, stay yo' ass right where you at!*" *I yelled.*

"*Vonka, let me explain!*" *he begged with his hands up, trying to reason with me.*

I knew it wasn't because he cared about what I was feeling at that moment, but simply that I held his life in my hands at that exact moment. If I chose for today to be his last day breathing, that would be it. This was exactly why I didn't do this love shit, because of no good ass niggas like this!

"Huh?" he asked. I guess I must have been talking out loud, but I just didn't give a fuck at this moment. I wanted to slap the fuck out of him right now as I watched Erick reach to grab his clothes.

"Don't you fucking move!" I yelled as I pointed the gun at him as he began to cry. I should kill his ass just for sitting here crying like he wasn't the one who was in here fucking my man.

"Shit, I must be mistaken, huh? You crying and shit like I was fucking your man. Well damn, my bad. I probably have been. I should be looking at this stupid muthafucka over here, huh?" I stated as he began to cry harder.

"I didn't know. He told me he was single," he sobbed as snot began to come out his nose about to make me throw up in my mouth. What grown ass man does all that fucking crying that snot comes out their nose? That's some nasty shit.

"If you don't stop all that bitch ass crying and wipe your fucking nose! Shit is disgusting!" I yelled as I looked over at Troy who had yet to say one word.

"So, when were you going to tell me that you didn't like what I had to offer, hmm?" I yelled.

"I love you, don't do this—" he started as I cocked the gun and shot in between him and his little boyfriend, causing him to cry out.

"I don't know, man. I don't know!" he yelled back as I nodded my head in response.

"You don't know, huh? Alright, get dressed and give me your

phones now!" I yelled as they scrambled around the room and gave them to me.

"I'll be downstairs waiting for y'all to come down. You got two minutes; make it quick," I stated in a calm and smooth tone as I walked out of the room to call Lena. She answered on the first ring surprisingly.

"I'm going to kill him, Lena. Get here, and get here fast," I stated in a calm tone, hanging up before she could respond at all.

I have never felt so stupid in my entire life, I thought as I paced back and forth as I heard the door open from upstairs as they made their way down the steps looking scared as hell. I looked over at his bitch ass boyfriend.

"Have a seat. You probably know where everything is at anyway since y'all drinking my wine and shit," I stated with a devious smirk.

"Hmmm okay," he stuttered as he continued to stand. He looked at the door when a knock resounded at the door.

"Y'all better shut up," I stated as I walked up to the door but still keeping them in my sight.

"Who is it?" I asked.

"Open the door, Vee," I heard Lena say as I rolled my eyes. I was not expecting her to get there that fast. I opened the door to see she had brought her strap with her just in case I needed her.

"What's going on, Vee, and who is that with the snot running down his face?" she asked with a confused expression coming across her face.

"Shit, I don't know. Why don't you ask Troy who that is," I stated as I shut the door behind her pointing my gun back at him.

"You know what? Let's cut all this shit short. Why you have to do me like this? You could have given me something!" I yelled as tears began to stream down my cheek as I began to break *down, so I knew it was only going to go left from there, and so did Lena. I watched her out of the corner of my eye walk slowly toward me.*

"Hey, get out of here now!" she yelled, and I watched his lover not think twice about leaving his ass, but I couldn't just let him go without nothing to remember me by. I pushed Lena away from me and pointed my gun back at him.

POW! POW!

Present

Just thinking about that day made my skin boil. I still didn't know how I was able to move on to Bronx after that shit. But obviously, I didn't kill his dumb ass, I definitely felt like I would have if I hadn't called Lena that day. She was definitely the calm one unless pushed, but all you had to do was poke my ass and you were awakening a sleeping bear. I didn't allow anybody to walk all over me anymore after that shit. We made our way to our cars, and I just hoped Bronx wasn't as stupid as Troy was because I was not going to be made a fool out of twice, and that was a promise.

"I HOPE YOU HAVE EVERYTHING PACKED AND READY TO go. Ain't nobody packing and moving your stuff, Lena." I heard Vonka yell. I continued to move around the room to get the rest of my things packed up and ready to go.

"I got this. I'm practically finished anyway," I yelled back as I placed the last strip of tape on the box in front of me. I walked into the bathroom to make sure that everything I had in the bathroom was all packed up and ready to go as I looked over into the mirror to get a good look at my attire and tighten my ponytail to make sure not a single piece of hair was out of place.

"Did you ask your new boo to help you move all this shit besides just looking to me for help? Did you forget you decided it was a good idea to stay on the sixth floor?" she asked with an attitude, hands on her hip and all.

"What boo?" I asked as I looked over my shoulder abruptly to meet her eyes.

As I watched her smile begin to rise with mischief finding its place in her eyes. "Bitch, don't play like you weren't out with Nash all night long a few nights back," she said with a laugh.

I wasn't even going to entertain her nonsense at the moment. So I walked around her to grab the box closest to the bed.

"That was all Bronx's doing. Plus, Nash invited his damn self. If you must know, he drove me crazy all damn day." I looked over to notice she wasn't following me out the room but was just staring at me like I was crazy.

"What?!"

"Don't what me! I don't know how stupid you think I am. But you're the one who came into the house at twelve o'clock at night a couple days ago. Plus, Bronx told me y'all went out and his ass didn't have any of the details. It just slipped my mind for a second, since all this bullshit has been going on to bring it up. So gon head and give me the tea, spill it."

"All we did was look at apartments, and then he asked me to grab something to eat because it was late. Thank you very much wit' cho nosy ass," I added with a smile while walking out of the room to avoid further conversations about that man, he already took up full residence in my mind.

I didn't need him being the topic of any and everything I talked about. He wouldn't be getting the chance to break me anyway, so it was really no reason to even entertain the idea of having his fine chocolate ass in between my thighs, behind it, or in my mouth. *Here I go again*. This was exactly why I didn't need his ass to be brought up. It was almost as if my heart couldn't get enough of being torn to shreds over and over again.

"Girl, please! So y'all went on a date?" she asked, following me out to the truck without one damn thing in her hand to help me.

"Umm, we are going to be here all damn day if you keep this up! Where is your box at?" I asked as I placed the box that was in my hands into the trunk.

"Don't ask me nothing until you answer the question. Plus, I'm not moving any of this shit. I'm waiting until Bronx get here so he can help you."

"It wasn't a date. He kissed me, but that was all," I stated in a rushed tone as I walked back into the house to grab the closest box to get some things done.

"Oh, hell no! What happened after that?" she shouted, following close behind me.

"Nothing else happened after that. I'm sure it was a mistake. Even if it wasn't, it will not be happening again!"

"I really don't know who you're trying to fool. What type of friend would I be to let you pass up on a good guy like this? I know you remember what you said to me when I tried that with Bronx after that messy situation with Troy," Vonka stated while taking the box out of her hand to place it on the couch behind her.

"You're really slowing down our progress, but if you must know, I remember exactly what I said, but you and I are two different people."

"Two different people my ass! You know exactly what Troy did to me. Now, tell me that you wouldn't have marked off all men after the trifling shit he did. Now Quran, Jason, Mike, Bryson... well, you know what dammit you get the point! They were not worthy of what you have to offer," she stated as I stared out into space because I just wanted to focus on all of the men who did not mean me any good.

How else was I going to stick with the fact that Nash just wasn't the one for me? "I hear you. I just don't think I'm ready to take the chance that this could be another mistake I would be making yet again."

"Who says that all of those guys were mistakes? I play a lot, but not on this. Those experiences taught you something. Bitch, use them. Don't let yourself miss out on the best experiences that life can bring you. If I had not given Bronx a chance, I wouldn't have been able to experience real love." I didn't know what had come over her, but I couldn't allow this little speech to deter me, but the thought wouldn't hurt too much.

"I'm going to call Bronx to see where his ass is at. I wasn't playing about not helping move any of these boxes. I didn't even move my own shit!" she laughed while trying to dodge the pillow I had just pulled off the couch to throw her way.

Bronx

My phone continued to ring over and over again as I ran over to the bleachers to grab it because everybody knew I had practice around this time, so they knew not to call because I wasn't going to answer unless it was a damn emergency. With the way this phone has been going off, somebody had better died. The minute I looked at the caller ID and the call was private, I just knew it was going to be some bullshit.

"Aye, who is this?" I asked as I walked over to have a seat on the bleachers to grab my water bottle.

"You know exactly who this is? I have your fucking daughter! You should have picked up on the first call. You with that bitch or something?" she yelled as I put the phone down to calm my nerves. I was really getting tired of this bullshit. This was exactly why you didn't fuck with groupies. I fucked up at the beginning of Vonka's and my relationship, and now this female came around a year later talking about this was my child, and that she was going to take it to the papers and let them know I was a deadbeat father, which was completely ridiculous since I didn't find out until two months ago, and I still hadn't told Lavonka about this shit. I just wanted to make sure it was true before I went and pissed her off. Because when she was mad, she was a whole new female once she felt like she had been played, which is more the reason why I needed to tell her ass before this chick told her. That shit wouldn't be any good for me.

"Hello! Do you hear me talking to you?" she yelled, pulling me out of my thoughts.

"I don't know who you think you're talking to, but you better pipe your tone down when you're on the phone with me. Now, what do you need, Aleece?" I asked as she smacked her teeth on the other line.

"Your daughter misses you, so when are you coming to see her. She also needs some more pampers and milk," she added in her typical fashion of entitlement like shit was just supposed to happen because she wanted it.

"Well, she is going to continue to miss me until you get me a paternity test! You calling my phone private all damn day ain't changing shit!" I yelled as everyone in the gym turned to look at me. I hopped up. I had forgotten where I was. This was exactly why I didn't answer any fucking calls while I was at practice.

"You are such a fucking deadbeat! You know just like I do this is your daughter!" she yelled, becoming irate.

"Actually, I don't think so. When you are able to send me the address and time to the doctor to get a paternity test done, that is when yo' ass can call me and get anything. Now, because this baby is innocent, I'm going to send my homie to drop of the milk and pampers," I stated in a tired voice because this situation was getting old as hell.

I hung up before she could say shit else. I knew exactly what her game was. She was trying to be in my presence because she thought we were going to be a family, and even if Lavonka left my ass over this shit, I surely wouldn't be with her. I thought as Nash walked over to me laughing, because he knew everything that was going on.

"Let me guess, Aleece's crazy ass?" I looked at him like who the hell else, and he burst out into laughter.

"I told yo' ass that night something was wrong with her, but did you want to take my advice? Hell nah," he stated as I nodded.

"You right, and I'm regretting that shit now," I

responded as we started heading toward the locker room to grab our stuff.

"Have you told Lavonka what's going on?" he asked as he grabbed our stuff out of the lockers.

"Hell nah, I'm going to tell her when we get back from this away game. Vee has been busier than a muthafucka. It's hard for me to catch a second with her. Since they opened this studio, she got more meetings with the bank than I've ever heard of!" I added because I missed her nagging ass, but I was not going to lie, it definitely gave me an excuse for why I hadn't told her what's really up.

"Didn't you offer to front her studio?" he asked as we walked out of the gym, heading toward our cars.

"Hell yeah, but she was talking about some shit like she wanted this to be something she accomplished on her own, so I didn't fight her on it," I added with a shrug.

"True. Well, you better tell Vonka what's going on because that bitch is crazy, and you know I don't like calling females out of their name, but that's no female. She a full-blown barracuda." This man was an utter fool.

"Man, I'm gonna tell her because if anybody knows how Vee can get, it's me," I added as I threw my bag into the trunk of my car.

"So what's up with Alena?" he asked as I turned around to see he was looking at me expectantly.

"Shit, I don't know to be real. But by the way she came in the house yesterday, I would assume you know more than I do," I added with a straight face. "You ain't just fuckin around, are you? I can't have you doing that shit to my girl's best friend. Do you know how long I would hear about this shit?" I asked as he laughed with a smirk coming across his face.

"Nah, she crazy as hell herself, but that's definitely my wife. But she got some issues to work through. I'm gonna sit back and let her come to me." I nodded, understanding exactly what he meant because you couldn't make anyone ready to receive love if they didn't want to receive it.

"Well, shit, let me get to this damn house since this is our last night before we gotta go tomorrow." We dapped each other up as I headed toward my car to make my way to the house when my phone started ringing again. I glanced down at the screen to see Vee was calling me as I instantly answered.

"Where you at, baby?" she asked as the smooth sweet sounds of her voice came through the radio of the car.

"I'm headed to the house from practice. Why? You need me to pick something up for you before I get there?" I asked as I heard her mumbling to someone else in the background that I was sure was Alena.

"So, what's up with your little friend that you didn't get to finish telling me about because we were preoccupied," she stated in a sultry voice. If I recalled correctly, her legs were wrapped around my waist all night.

"What about him, Vee?" I asked because I hated being in the middle of this shit.

"Don't play dumb! He say something about Alena today?" she asked.

I just knew this was going to happen. This was precisely why I told him he needed to leave her alone because if this shit didn't work out, she was going to bring up this conversation continuously.

"What I tell you about talking to me like that? If you want something, talk to me like you got some fuckin' sense, Vee," I stated as I heard her smack her teeth on the other end. I didn't know why women liked to do that shit when they had an attitude about what was said to them that they couldn't say shit back to but answered with a smack of their teeth.

"I hear you, so what he say?" she asked in an excited voice.

"Calm yo' happy ass down. He just said he gonna give her her space because Nash knows she needs it, but basically, he really feeling her. That's about it, but next time you're going to need to tell Lena to ask that man if she wants to know anything else," I stated as I made my way into the neighborhood.

"Okay! Well bye, that's all I wanted to know. Love you," she stated quickly while hanging up before I could get another word out.

I just cruised as I thought back to that night I got myself into that situation. I wished I could take that back every time I think about it.

Last year

"Man, I'm just going to go back to my room. I've had enough of the festivities I'm sure my girl ready to FaceTime me," I stated with pride because I had one of the most beautiful, independent, and confident women out here.

"Lavonka's ass is good without you for another hour. She

knows you out with yo' boys," Mark stated as the rest of the guys laughed. I looked over at Nash who shrugged his shoulders because he didn't want no part of it.

"Aight, one more hour, and then I'm going to my damn room to talk to my girl," I added as we headed to the next club when this Spanish chick who looked like a Jennifer Lopez look-alike with long auburn hair going down her back eyes latched onto mine.

"Leave it alone, bruh, she fine as hell, but you got a good girl at home," I heard Nash say as he placed his hand on my shoulder to admire the beautiful ass woman before us.

"I'm not worried about her. Nothing wrong with looking," I stated as I brought my glass of Henny up to my lips.

"Mmmhmm, but it always the ones that look like that that's crazy as all hell," he stated as we made our way from the bar to the VIP section that was marked off just for us.

We had been chilling for a minute, listening to music, when I stood up to say my goodbyes because going out had never been my scene. The minute I had made it out of the VIP, homegirl from earlier was right at my side with a tight body-hugging red dress that went down to the bottom of her ass.

"Leaving so soon?" she asked in a sultry tone.

"Yeah, my girl is waiting for me to call her," I stated as I continued to head toward the door with her right on my heels.

"Oh, so you have a girlfriend?" she asked while following me out.

"Yeah, I do," I stated, trying to brush her off as best as I could when I felt her hand slide down to grip my dick in my pants.

"Looks to me like you want to be with me instead," she stated as she began to nibble on my neck.

My hands began to slide down to her ass as I gripped it with both hands. I hadn't realized she had pulled me into the bathroom. I locked the door behind her as I turned her over and slipped my hands under her dress. I lifted it up from her body to find she wasn't wearing any panties.

Present

Shit, just thinking about that night killed my mood, because if I would have avoided her that night, I wouldn't be going through the bullshit I am now. I knew I told Nash that I would tell Vee after the out of town game, but I just knew that when she found out, she was going to leave my ass, and I couldn't deal with that right now. She was the only person in a long time that had been just about me and made just for me. *I'm going to have to figure this out before she does*, I thought while pulling into the driveway to a moving truck outside the house. Damn, I forgot Lena was moving out today. That's probably why Vonka was really calling me with her lazy ass. The minute I stepped out the car, the front door burst open with Vonka heading toward me.

"How was practice?" she asked as she swung her arms around my neck and leaned her head back for a kiss. I knew exactly what was up as I slid my hand down to grip her ass.

I leaned down to slip my tongue into her mouth, causing a moan to slide between her lips. I pulled back before she got something started that her ass was going to have to finish.

"I'm good, baby, just tired. Why? What you need?"

"Why you always think I need something?"

"Because you always do, now what's up? Because I

know you haven't been moving nothing, huh?" I asked as Lena walked out the house with a box in her hand.

"Hell no! She ain't moved not one damn thing! And I don't even have that much shit here. The rest of it I need to get from Quran's house," she stated with a laugh as she placed the box that was in her hands into the back of the moving truck.

"You ain't have to tell me that." I laughed as I moved out the way of her outreached hand.

I felt my phone begin to vibrate. The minute I looked down to see private, I knew it wasn't anyone but Aleece's crazy ass calling me back to back like I hadn't just talked to her. I looked up to notice Vonka was staring at me like I had lost my mind.

"Who is that?" she asked with a smile.

I knew that shit wasn't nothing but a front. She wanted me to say the wrong answer, so she could show her ass out here. But she wasn't ready for the truth, or maybe she was, but I sure as hell wasn't. I looked over at her with a smirk as I put my phone back into my pocket. "Mmmhmm, let me see," she stated as she started heading my way.

I don't know what the hell I was going to do. I was contemplating dropping this shit and fucking my screen all up because everybody knew that iPhones were fragile as fuck. But then, she really was gon' know what was up. My phone started going off again. Before I could even get it up to look at it, she was snatching the phone out of my hand. If I thought I was going to be fucked before, I could kiss all that ass she was carrying goodbye. Because Aleece's ass was about to run it down like a muthafucka.

"Who the fuck is this calling my man phone!" Vonka yelled. I was just standing over here shitting bricks as I watched her expression change, and her face turned red.

"Oh, you almost got Bronx fucked up just now. Here he goes." She laughed as she brought the phone back over to me.

I looked down to see Nash's ass was on the phone. I was definitely going to have my ass in somebody's church Sunday and even Wednesday for Bible study. I knew it wasn't anybody but God that just saved me right now. Because I just knew I was going to be living outside in one of my cars because I wasn't staying in anybody's hotel so that everybody could be in my damn business wondering why I wasn't home with my girl.

"Bruh, what the hell ya got going on over there?" I heard Nash ask as I grabbed my bag out the car.

I yelled over to Vonka and Lena, letting them know I would be back to help. I just wanted to put my bag in the house.

"Man, Aleece's ass has been blowing up my phone since practice. I'm just tired of this bullshit."

"I told you that you better tell Vonka what's up because that girl is unstable, and you know that!" he yelled.

I wasn't even pissed, because he was right. I knew this was going to explode in my face at some point if I didn't get this shit together and quick.

"Enough about me and my bullshit. You coming over to help move Lena into her new apartment?"

"I don't know about that. She ain't gon' be feeling that."

"Shit, help is help. You can't pay her no damn attention. Bruh, you know Vonka's ass ain't doing nothing but running her mouth."

He laughed because he knew like I did how true the shit was. I loved my baby to the end, but she was one of the laziest muthafuckas I'd ever met. If it wasn't necessary to help with something, she wasn't doing it.

"Yeah, I know. Give me ten minutes."

"Aight." I didn't know what I was going to do about Aleece's crazy ass, but I needed to get that paternity test done and quick.

NASH

I DIDN'T KNOW WHAT MY PROBLEM WAS. I JUST couldn't take a hint when it was given. This woman drove me completely crazy with her ungrateful ass. I took her on a full-blown date and she got there and acted like a complete child. I started pulling up to the actual apartment building since Bronx called letting me know they had gotten everything packed up and were heading this way. The minute I stepped a foot outside of the car, I saw her bent over in her truck. I watched three women walk up to her. I could see a frown coming across her face as I watched the interaction from afar, just trying to make sure everything was cool as I made my way toward them.

"Everything cool, Alena?" I asked as I watched the skinny big-headed girl look over at me with a lick of her lips.

"Yeah, everything is cool," she responded as she pulled her body closer to mine. *I don't know what she is up to, but I have no problem playing along with her fine ass*, I thought when the girl that looked to be the leader of the group looked over at me again as she turned her body toward me to address me.

"So, you like fat bitches too, huh?" she asked. When I heard a laugh escape Lena's lips, I just knew she didn't find shit funny that homegirl said as I wrapped my arms around her waist to pull her in closer to my body.

I leaned down to grip her chin as I turned her to face me. While leaning down to kiss her lips ever so softly, I could hear smacking and loud breathing. I pulled back to look over at the three girls who had envy all over their faces.

"You ladies have a good rest of your day. I know y'all got better shit to do than be concerned with what my woman is doing all day. So, take y'all tow down version of the Supremes asses on," I stated as I watched their mouths drop open like they couldn't believe what I had just said.

I turned back to look at Alena who had calmed down some since the comment. "So what's left to be moved, baby?" I asked as her whole expression changed.

"I just have a couple boxes left that we can take in after the trash leaves," she stated in a giddy voice.

"Bitch, this isn't over, and don't think that for one minute," I heard the skinny one announce as she walked over to the car she drove up in.

"You cool?" I asked as she closed her eyes, trying to control her temper in the process.

"Yeah, I'm good. Seems like you always show up at

just the right time." She laughed more so out of frustration.

"I guess you can say that, but you always got something going on. You got me worried about you."

"Yeah, it sure seems that way, but what are you doing here?" she asked as she leaned against the moving truck.

"Bronx told me y'all was moving today, so I figured why not offer a hand?" I added with a smirk as I placed my hand on my chest.

"Mmmhmm, how I know you're not out here being a stalker, trying to catch cheap feels and kisses. I think you were feeling that kiss more than you should have been," she added with a smirk as she turned around not to meet my eyes while grabbing one of the boxes out the back of the truck.

I walked up behind her to wrap my arms around her waist to show her that it was definitely real to me. I felt her take a deep breath in feeling me, thick and long, against all that ass she had toting back there.

"Maybe I am, but what you gon' do about that?" I whispered in a smooth tone in her ear as a moan slipped from in between her lips.

I knew she was feeling me. I would never understand why it was always such a game to her. *I figured if I gave her some time and space that it would help her come to her senses, but I was wrong about that. I needed to show her this was real to me and that I wasn't like every dude that, when shit wasn't working out, they fell back. Because that definitely was not the case. Oh, she was gon' figure that out this time around.* She instantly pulled out of my arms while turning around to place the box that was in her hands into mine.

"If you came to help, I'm gonna need you to stop playing around. I'm not going to be out here all night. Thanks again for the help," she added as she backed up away from me to head inside the apartment building like her ass was on fire.

I knew she was feeling me, but she just needed a push. Dammit, I just didn't need any other types of distractions, because her beautiful ass required all my attention at the moment if I had plans on marrying her.

"So you not gon' tell me the apartment number?" I yelled as I walked into the apartment behind her laughing.

Alena

I didn't know what the hell I was thinking letting him kiss me like that. Where the hell was Lavonka when you needed her ass? She and Bronx were probably somewhere fucking. But I was glad he showed up at the moment he did because I didn't know what would have happened when that little skinny bitch and her two ugly ducklings walked up on me like they wanted a problem. Now, would I have had a few cuts and bruises? Maybe, but I wasn't going to be the only one leaving fucked up. I didn't know what problem that girl had with me seeing as I hadn't talked to Quran since his bitch ass came over to Vonka's house, trying to choke me the hell out. I just couldn't catch a damn break. If it was not one thing, it was another. Then I had Nash's fine ass down my back. All I needed to do was stay away from this man and all his fine ass glory and smooth talking. I thought it had worked last time when I told him I didn't want his ass, and he hadn't been bothering me. But the look he just gave me outside said otherwise, and that shit worried me more than I wanted to admit. The smell of Ironclad by Avon & Kenneth Cole caressed my senses like a sweet symphony. I felt his presence before he even got one word out.

"So, you wasn't gonna tell me where to take this box?" he asked in his usual cocky tone.

"It looks like you found it well enough without me," I added in a smart tone as I walked into the apartment to move the boxes from just being all over the place.

"So where you want it? Or does it not matter?" he asked as he looked around the room to notice I had just placed boxes anywhere.

"What you trying to say? I'm just putting shit anywhere. I don't need your opinion—" I started as I watched him set the box in his hands to the side without a word as he shut the door behind him and began to stalk toward me as I backed myself into the wall.

"What are you doing?" I asked now that he was all in my personal space.

"You just love fucking with me, huh?" he stated as he gripped my waist while lifting me from the floor to put me against the wall as my legs instinctively wrapped around his waist.

His lips latched onto mine in an urgent manner as he slipped his tongue into my mouth. Nash placed me back on my feet as he gripped the ends of my shirt to pull it over my head, as we helped each other get out of all our clothes. At this moment, I was happy as hell that I had my bed in this damn apartment. Regardless of the fact that it was just laying on the ground. The minute we made our way to the bed, he began to send earth-shattering kisses to every crevice of my body. When he finally made it to my clit, he began teasing me with slow licks and slurps of my juices as he began to suck my clit into his mouth.

"Mmmm, don't stop!" I moaned out as he continued to make love to my pussy with his tongue. "Ohhhh shiiiitttt!" I screamed out as I came harder than I had ever cum with any man.

To think, his ass was just getting started. When I looked up, he kissed back up my body as he slipped his tongue back into my mouth. I feasted on the taste of my essence in his mouth. I felt him lean back as he kicked his basketball shorts off. He leaned back to stroke his nine-inch dick that was standing straight up. He stared deep into my eyes as I licked my lips and nodded, letting him know I wanted everything he had to offer me. I felt the thick head of his dick probing my center as he finally slid into my tight center with slow and precise strokes, hitting my g-spot with every stroke.

"Whose shit is this, Lena?" he groaned into my ear as he began to deliver powerful strokes.

"Mmmm yoooouurrrs!" I moaned out as he flipped me over suddenly. I arched my back with perfection as I began to throw it back at him making my ass clap in the process.

"Damnnn!" I heard him groan out as I began to tighten my box around his dick, trying to milk him for everything he had in him.

I felt a sharp pull when he pulled my hair, bringing my upper body off the bed as he began to pound my box out in fast strokes while nibbling on my neck. Turning me on even more, he wrapped his hand around my neck to choke me a little bit as I screamed out and creamed all over his pipe. I felt him cumming right along with me as we fell onto the mattress in exhaustion until I heard something in the living room. It almost sounded like Lavonka.

"Shit," I whispered as I hopped out of bed to hear Lavonka talking shit about how I hadn't moved that much shit into the apartment.

I slapped Nash's leg to get his attention as he turned over to look at me with a smirk. I didn't know how I was going to get his shit out the living room without her noticing it if she hadn't already.

"Please be quiet. I'm going to get her to go outside with me, and you put your shit back on and come back in here and act like you're putting something together for me!" I whispered as he smirked at me like he had something up his sleeve.

"Aight cool, but if I do this, your ass is going to cut all this bullshit out and let me show you what a real man is! Agreed?" he stated as he looked me into my eyes waiting for an answer as I threw on the last remaining clothes I had in the room with us.

"Alright. Alright," I whispered back with a smack of my teeth as he leaned forward to kiss my lips while pulling on his boxers. I did not need to be flustered when I walked out of this room, I pulled the door open to walk right into Vonka, who was looking at me like I was crazy.

"What you been doing? I know yo' ass wasn't waiting for us to help move the rest of your shit while you took naps?" she stated, walking behind me as I kicked Nash's basketball shorts under the table, hoping he would be able to find them when I got Vonka out of this damn apartment.

"Girl, please, but let's go see what's left. Where is Bronx? Is he outside?" I asked as I walked out the apartment with her hot on my heels.

"Bitch, I don't know what your problem is, but I'm going to figure that shit out!" she stated as I walked out to the truck to see Bronx was grabbing the last of the boxes.

"The question is what were you doing? Y'all left forty-five minutes ago to get trash bags and never came the hell back. I know there is a Walmart right up the street, so what happened to you?" I asked as she burst into laughter.

"I'm not even gonna lie to you, girl, because you like a sister to me. Bitch, I was getting some dick. You know I can't go long without that thang over there stroking me! I know you see I be about to die when he leaves for away games! I gotta get it while I can!" she yelled as I burst out laughing at her crazy self because I knew she was as serious as a heart attack.

"What y'all laughing about?" I heard Bronx ask as

he walked into the building with the last bits of my nonsense.

"Just this crazy heffa you call your girlfriend. Something is wrong with her." I laughed nervously as I watched Nash start walking toward us with a screwdriver that I didn't know where he even got the shit from. I looked over at Vonka who was looking at me like I had left her out of the loop.

"Lena didn't tell me you were here!" she added with a laugh as she walked around both Bronx and me to speak.

"Get fucked up, Vee," I heard Bronx state in a no-nonsense tone while walking into the apartment.

"I'm just saying hi. Is that okay with you?" she responded as she followed him into the apartment.

"I went and asked one of her neighbors if they had a screwdriver since she ain't got no tools. I was trying to put her shelf together for her since she had about brought almost everything in here." Damn, he was smarter than I gave him credit for because my idea was probably more unbelievable.

I just didn't want to explain what this was to Lavonka, because I still didn't know and didn't want to give it too much more thought.

"I forgot I needed that. Thanks," I responded as Vonka turned to look at me with a surprised expression.

"What?" I asked as I headed to the back to start taking out some of the things I had purchased for my new apartment.

"Don't what me. I know his ass wasn't back here fixing

shit. The only thing he was back here doing was wearing your ass out. Y'all ain't fooling nobody," Vonka stated as she burst out laughing at my surprised expression.

"Whatever," I stated not even going to feed into her mess, because that's exactly what she wanted.

"Don't get upset with me, bitch. I ain't the only one walking bowlegged around this bitch."

I couldn't stand this heffa, I thought as I burst out laughing because this girl was horrible.

"Man! Just help me put this stuff up!" I laughed as I threw one of the free towels from my bag at her.

"I'm trying to help you out. You ain't gotta date the man. Bronx started out as my fuck buddy. Now look at us. That's my baby, and I wouldn't change a thing about him. So just have fun!" she stated as she started pulling my stuff out of the boxes to help me put all this mess away.

It was crazy thinking that she just might be right. I was cool with just sex, but nothing else, and I needed to make sure he was aware of that.

Later that Night

Lavonka and Bronx had finally left, leaving me alone with this fine ass man. I knew she knew exactly what I was trying to do earlier. I kept them here as long as I could to avoid this conversation.

"So, are you done playing?" I heard him ask from behind me as I shut the front door.

"What are you talking about?" I asked, trying to play naïve. I looked over my shoulder at him, and a chuckle slipped between his lips.

"I guess that's a no, huh," he stated as he took long

strides toward me, lifting me off my feet and placing me on my island, so that we were at eye level.

"I'm going to be real with you, this is real for me. I think you're it. The problem is getting you to realize that shit, which is why I been staying out your way. But now I see that was the wrong approach. You like when a man just asserts himself in your life, so you got it, baby. Now tonight, I'm going to let you sit on that, but tomorrow, be ready by six. We got plans," he stated, leaving me speechless.

I always had a weakness for a man that could put you in your place, and his ass just did that smooth as hell.

"You hear me?" he asked as he leaned in to peck my lips nice and smooth.

I nodded my head as he pulled back and started to head for the door before shooting over his shoulder.

"Dress casual." I still hadn't said one word since he first started talking as he shut the door behind him.

I hopped off the counter to lock the door with a quickness, just in case his ass decided to come back. I couldn't deal with him too much more in my space. Shit, now that I thought of it, he just created a damn date without my permission. This was precisely what happened when you met a man with a big dick and a mean stroke game. Yo' ass became dickmatized and couldn't speak one lick. *Now, I didn't have a choice but to be ready by six tomorrow*, I thought as I heard a knock at my door. I knew his ass didn't come back. He was already making demands and shit. What else could he want? Because he surely wasn't getting any more pussy.

"Who is it?" I yelled, and he didn't say nothing back as I looked out the peephole to see he had it covered. This man was always playing.

I pulled the door open without a second thought. "What do you need now——" I started as the rest of the words I was getting ready to say got stuck in my mouth as Quran stepped around me and into my house.

I finally came to my senses as I turned around to see his ass had made himself at home on my couch like he lived here.

"Excuse me? Get the hell out. Yo' ass wasn't invited in here!" I yelled, trying to keep my voice down since this was my first day being in this damn apartment, and I didn't need everyone in the building knowing my business.

"Man, baby, just shut the door, and let me talk to you for a second," he stated, not moving one muscle, so I picked up my phone to text Nash.

Nash, you left your shorts here. I need you to come back and get them now!

I just hoped he understood exactly what I was saying because I didn't have my gun near me to shoot this man if he got a little happy with his hands, which he always ended up doing because he couldn't get his way with me.

"What do you want, Quran, and how the hell did you find out where I live?" I asked, firing off question after question.

"Will you sit yo' ass down and relax, damn! I ain't gon' bite," he added with a smirk as he leaned back on the couch.

I walked around to sit on the opposite side as he leaned on his knees. "When you gon' stop with this dumb bullshit. Yeah, I fucked up, and I apologized. I don't even fuck that bitch anymore," he chided as a giggle slipped through my lips.

This muthafucka here just made me revert to somebody else when I was naturally a calm, cool, collective type of girl. I didn't know if he thought he was talking to an idiot, but he had the right one.

"Is that right? Well, why this bucket head ass hoe keeps showing up anywhere I'm at ready to be fucked up, huh?" I retorted as the smirk that was once on his face dropped and changed into an angry expression.

"Who the fuck is you getting smart with?" he stated as he tilted his head to the side.

"Shoot, let me guess, you and me the only muthafuckas in here," I stated in a calm voice as I stormed over to the door and held it open.

"You know what? Get yo' ass up and get out my house! Don't come back, because there will never be another you and me," I stated with a serious expression as Nash walked right through the open door as I heard Quran chuckle.

I felt hands gripping my chin bringing me back to look him in his eyes.

"You straight?" he asked as I nodded with him leaning down to tongue me down. I forgot Quran was still in the room until I heard him speak up to let his presence be known.

"Oh, so this the shit you looking for, huh?" He laughed as he hopped up from the couch and headed our way. I looked up to see that Nash had pulled me behind him as Quran walked by with a devious smirk coming across his face.

"I'm gon' catch you around, Lena. Believe that shit," he promised as he walked past Nash and out of the apartment. I didn't know what the hell he meant by that, but I was getting tired of all of his little pop-ups like he wasn't the one who ruined our relationship. I wished he would do me the favor of just letting me live my life. Not to mention, this was my first time moving into this apartment, and I already felt uneasy about being here alone.

"Where your extra blankets at?" he asked while closing and locking the door behind him.

I hadn't noticed he had even left out of the apartment. I guess he went to make sure Quran didn't do any extra shit since he was in the business of being a complete stalker now.

"Uhh, in that box over by the counter. You know you don't have to stay, right? I'll be fine," I stressed.

"Yeah, I know I don't, but I'm going to," he responded as he spread out the blanket he had found in the box over the couch and grabbed a pillow as well to get comfortable.

"So, you're just going to sleep on my furniture?" I asked with a small smile as he looked over his shoulder at me.

"Yeah, where else am I going to sleep at?" he responded as I grabbed his hand to pull him off the couch.

In my eyes, he definitely earned some pussy for

handling the situation the way he did. I pulled him toward the back where my bed was set up with their help from earlier. I didn't believe no other words needed to be said. At this point, he had me. Now, the question was what was he going to do with that information when he got it?

NASH

I was surprised as hell she had let me stay the night with her, but then again, she did have ole boy just popping up like he was still running shit. I knew her ex popping up made her more uncomfortable than she was letting on, which is exactly why I'm ready for her to stop playing, and let me show her what you get when you fuckin' with a real man.. But I didn't have a doubt in my mind that she was going to be my wife if things went the way I wanted them to. I headed to the locker room to grab my stuff so I could get ready for everything I had planned tonight for her.

"So what you got planned?" Bronx asked as he grabbed his bag out of his locker.

"I'm thinking like a salsa class and then take her to dinner, but it's a picnic type deal slash boat ride. You think she will like that?" I asked, hoping he would give me the go with the idea.

"Hmm, the salsa shit is cool, but they dancers, man. They already are doing shit like that. You gotta think a little bit more outside of the box, like a scavenger hunt or some shit," he responded while headed out to the parking lot to head out. Since tonight would be the last night with the ladies before we had to go to an away game tomorrow, I was sure he had something up his sleeve with Vonka too.

"I GUESS YOU RIGHT. AIGHT, MAN," I stated as we dapped each other up, going our separate ways. I needed to show her why giving me her heart for safe-keeping was worth it. As a thought popped into my head, I pulled my phone out to call the one person who I knew could help me make this the perfect night for her. Phase one of showing her what real love was.

6:00PM

Alena

It was six o'clock as I looked at my appearance in the mirror to make sure the outfit I was wearing wasn't too underdressed. As I looked in the mirror, I saw that the sweater dress and Vans I decided to wear looked just right. I decided to lay down all my baby hair and place it into a low ponytail. I was just utterly anxious because he wouldn't tell me where we were going, so now I didn't know if I was appropriately dressed or not. *But, oh well, if I wasn't, it was all his fault, and I wasn't going to feel no type of way about it*, I thought as I heard my phone ding signaling that I had a text message. I rushed to grab it, knowing it was Nash probably saying he was outside, but usually, he came upstairs, so he must have had something special down there. I looked to see it was a text with a cute quote attached.

Live like there's no midnight - Cinderella

I smiled down at the text as another one came through, letting me know to make my way to the front of the building because a night of surprises was ahead. I grabbed a small jacket and my purse as I locked up my apartment to head out front, and there was a carriage waiting out front for me, but no Nash.

"What is he up to?" I stated as the coachman hopped out the cart to open the door for me while handing me a card with another quote on it that read,

There isn't anything I wouldn't do for you, 'cause you got a friend in me- Toy Story. Reach under the seat, we wouldn't be best friends without one of these.

I leaned down as I reached for whatever he placed under the chair when I came across a box. The minute I pulled it open, there was a Pandora bracelet with a best friend charm hanging from it with our initials. I smiled at how much effort he was putting into this first date because I was used to just going to a movie and dinner and then back to his or my apartment because they all felt they had earned some pussy for spending fifty dollars for a date. I felt the carriage slow down in front of a salon. The door was opened for me as I headed inside to the front desk to be handed yet another card that read,

One look at your smile, & I could see the light shining every- where —Aladdin. Get ready to be pampered from your head to your feet. Jill will be there to help you out, and know she is my cousin.

. . .

I LAUGHED because that was exactly what I was thinking. *I wish he would have brought me to a salon to have some girl he used to mess with playing hairdresser in my head,* I thought when a dainty chocolate woman with big doe eyes and a bright smile approached me,

"I'm going to assume you're Alena! Hi, I'm Jill. We know you don't have too much time on your hands, so we are gonna get you in and out. Makeup and all! He thought this well out. You must be special. My cousin ain't ever asked me to do none of this before for nobody," she stated as she dragged me into a chair to wash my hair.

"You don't have to lie to me. He probably has had tons of girls around," I responded trying to laugh off the unwanted jealousy that was coursing through my body.

I closed my eyes as she began to massage my scalp, causing my eyes to almost roll to the back of my head. I loved to get my hair washed. That was the best part about getting your hair done, and she had hands of an angel. The minute she was finished washing my hair, she wrapped my hair up in a towel while bringing me over to her station.

"So, what do you want to be done? Blow out, wand curls, natural curls?" she asked.

"I'm going to try my hand at a blowout," I responded as she went to work on my head as two more girls walked up and began to give me a natural look with my makeup and another was doing my nails giving me a classic French tip. Almost forty-five minutes later, she gave me a mirror to look at my transformation, and to say I was looking like a brand-new woman was an understatement.

"Thanks, ladies. I love it!" I beamed.

Everyone else walked away as Jill stopped me from leaving with a smile.

"You're the only woman I have ever met that my cousin has stated that he wanted to be with in this way in a long time," she responded with a suddenly sad smile. I wanted to question the look that came across her face, but she instantly perked up and ushered me out the door with a new note in my hand with instructions not to open until my next destination. I was still in awe of how much effort he had put into this date, and this note card was burning a hole in my hand throughout the whole ride to this mystery place. I didn't know what this man was up to, but I was just going to play along. The door opened for me as I hopped out the car to head toward the door of the boutique as I headed into the shop.

"Alena?" the agent asked.

"Yup, that's me!" I responded as she led me to the private section in the back of the boutique. The minute I looked up, she brought in a velvet burgundy dress with a split that went up the thigh, and an all-black dress with a low dip in the back.

"Definitely the burgundy one!" I laughed as she nodded in agreement while bringing out a pair of all-black stilettos. Once I had changed into the dress, I walked over to the mirror and had to do a double take. I knew I was a good-looking girl, but I rarely got the chance to dress up like this unless I was going to an awards show or something to perform when I used to be a background dancer. The woman walked back in with another card letting me know that I was okay to read it. She led me back out the boutique and to the carriage. I just hoped this next stop was our last stop because I was ready to see him and thank him for everything he had done to make this date unique. Plus, I was impatient as hell. I looked down at the card to see what it read.

You're the one I've been looking for -The Little Mermaid. I know your ass is getting impatient. This is the last stop. You just have one more gift.

Nervous wasn't exactly how I would explain the way I was feeling right now as we pulled up to a park that led to an unknown ending.

"This is the last stop, little lady." I heard the coachman announce as he opened the door for me and held my hand to help me out the cart. I looked over to my left to see Nash standing under this archway that led down a brick path as I smiled. He was looking like a whole meal in his three-piece gray suit. It looked like it had been tailored to fit each and every one of the muscles in his body. I knew he knew I was checking him out as his deep brown eyes began to light up with lust and amusement. I watched him lick his lower lip out of purely a natural habit as he began to take strides toward me to bring me to the last part of the surprise I suppose.

"This was all so beautiful. You didn't have to do all of this. I would have been fine with dinner and a movie or something," I added bashfully, knowing damn well I was tired of that same old nonsense, but I would have sounded ungrateful as hell if I would have burst out saying 'Damn, I glad you didn't try and take me on a fifty-dollar date'. A giggle slipped through my lips as he looked over at me with his eyebrow instinctively going up.

"What's so funny?" he asked with a smirk coming across his face.

"Oh nothing, but this was really something, especially for a first date," I added as he stopped me where I was standing under the archway while handing me the last card.

"Read it," he stated as he watched me open the final card that read.

Let me share this whole new world with you- Aladdin. If you think this is something you can appreciate, then grab my hand and let me show you what real love can be. If not, I can have Ben take you home in the carriage and let you be.

I looked over the card as I thought about everything I'd been through. Did I have enough left in me to deal with another heartbreak? If this wasn't what I thought it was going to be, was I going to pass up on the one person who was meant for me?

"I'm willing to give this a try, but fuck up, and you gon' meet a whole new female," I stated in a smooth voice like I hadn't just threatened him.

I watched his facial expression to see if he would start acting crazy, like Quran would whenever he didn't get his way. Nothing changed as a smirk came across his face while wrapping his arms around my waist and pulling me into the comfort of his body.

"I got you, baby. That's not to say I won't make you mad or sad sometimes, but I definitely won't do it intentionally or stop trying to make you smile. I may be imperfect like any other person in this world, but I believe I was made imperfectly just for you," he proclaimed.

One lone tear slid down my face, not for the sweet words that he sang into my ear like a smooth harmony, but for the simple fact that I had lost yet again to love. I just hoped this time it was worth it. I felt his lips on my cheek as I closed my eyes to take in the moment as he kissed away every tear that broke away from the shield I had built around my heart.

"No more of that, woman. The night isn't over yet," he announced as he took my hand into his and lead me down the path to run right into a sight that almost left me breathless.

I took in the lights he had wrapped around all the trees harboring the quaint little table in the middle of the beauty with candlelight ready and burning on the table. From where I was standing, I could see that he had kept the meals warm for as long as he could as he pulled back my seat at the table. He uncovered my platter of chicken breast, rice, and cornbread. This was my favorite meal. I didn't know how he knew, because I had spent so much time trying to push him away that the time where you get to know each other almost didn't go as well. The minute he took a seat, he gripped both of my hands on the table.

"Bow your head, baby. I'm saying grace for us as well as the food," he responded in a nonchalant tone.

Once he was finished praying, he looked up at me with a bright smile.

"So, how did you plan all of this out?" I asked over almost a mouthful of chicken.

"I have my ways. Why you trying to come up with my secrets?" he added as I looked at him like he had lost his mind causing him to burst out into laughter. I don't know why he found me to be so funny when I was usually serious as hell.

"If you must know, Vonka helped out a little bit," he added with a smile. I should have known she knew something was up when she called me earlier asking me if I had shaved or not.

"Well, I love it. I've never had a man do anything like this for me. Also, your cousin was great. I like her, and she did amazing on my hair," I added.

"That she did, I knew you were going to pick that dress, and if I do say so myself, you look beautiful tonight." I placed my hand over my face as the blush I was trying to hold back took over on my face.

I felt his hand grip my hand, and the sounds of violins began to play "At Last" by Etta James. I hadn't even noticed they had come out into the opening with us as he helped me out my seat. He walked me away from the table as he placed my body into the comfort of his arms. I felt at home in his arms, and that's what scared me the most. I was giving this man every tool known to man to break me. This was everything I'd always wanted and frightened me at the same time. I felt his hand caress my back as I wrapped my arms around his neck, pulling myself as close as I could into his body. *I don't want to wake up if this is just a dream*, I thought as he began to place smooth kisses on my cheek. I pulled back to put a sensual kiss on his lips. I sucked on his bottom lip and then slipped my tongue into his mouth as he began to take control of the kiss. I felt his hands slide from the small of my back to my ass.

"Take me home," I announced as he pulled back with a surprised expression, almost defeated. "With you..." I finished as I watched a smile come across his face causing his dimples to make their way through.

"Aye, buddy, this dinner is over. 'Preciate you fam, but take care of this," he announced to the guy that was waiting away from the table.

I watched him pull out a stack of hundreds and placed them on the table while grabbing my hand and rushing back out toward the path.

"What happened to the gentleman I was just with all dinner?" I giggled as he looked back over at me with a smirk.

"You were at dinner with Nashoba, but you about to fuck with Nash now." Now this that type of shit I liked. I loved a man that could be a gentleman and put you in your place at the same time.

To say we made it to his house in record speed would be an understatement since we didn't take the carriage back. We just rode in his car instead. We pulled into his driveway, and I was completely surprised by everything I was seeing, I expected his house to look like Bronx's house with the modern detail. But he decided to take the typical family man house, almost like a ranch style house with the wrap around porch. I looked over at him to see he was looking at me to gauge my reaction. I didn't know what he expected, but I loved the house. This was always what I dreamed of. Out of Lavonka and me, I was the one who always talked about being a good wife with kids running around. I yearned for love more than she did, but I just couldn't catch a break. I couldn't find a good man if my life depended on it, which was what scared me about Nash because he was everything I prayed for when I was a little girl. I just knew this was too good to be true, but I was going to take a chance like every other time. Who knew? This could be my happy ending and God had seen everything I'd been through! I deserved this man. I looked out the window and then back over at him again with loving eyes.

"I love it. Now are you trying to show me a good time or what?" I asked as the look of adoration slipped from my face into pure lust as I licked my lower lip. I heard the doors unlock instantly as he turned from looking at me while coming around to my side of the car to open my door. The minute we stepped into the house, it was almost like a sense of urgency came over us. I threw my arms around his neck as he pulled my body into his. Nash pulled back as he took my hand into his, leading me to the back of the house. I was assuming to his room until we made it to the last door at the end of the hall. The minute we stepped into the room, it looked exactly how I expected. He had an all black and gray color scheme going throughout the whole room. In the center of the room was a California king size bed. He didn't have too many pieces of furniture. It was almost like he was waiting for someone to put the finishing touches on it. I almost forgot he was in room until he kissed the back of my neck.

"Make yourself comfortable," he whispered as he stepped out of the room.

I was trying to so hard not to let my nosiness take over as I walked over to his bed to get comfortable as I kicked my heels off. I unzipped the back of my dress as I let it drop to my feet. If I was going to give this a shot, I wasn't going to hold back. Instantly, music started to play throughout the room. It was the sounds of "Arch & Point" by Miguel. I laid across his bed in nothing but my black lace thong and bra as I heard the door creak open. The minute he walked in, he had two wine glasses in hand that he instantly set to the side. I bit my lower lip as he took his sweet time to make it to the bed. He leaned in between my thighs. Kissing from my feet up to my center, he paid close attention to every curve and crevice of my body to make sure he didn't miss an inch. I felt his hands pull my thong down my legs. I instantly felt a cool breeze hit my clit, causing me to moan out. I felt his tongue begin to tease my bud, and then he pulled back with a smirk coming across his face.

"Don't stop," I moaned out.

"Where you want me, baby?" I heard him ask as he began to nibble on my thighs closest to the one place I really wanted him.

Without any words, I took two fingers and slipped them into my mouth and slid them in between my lips.

"This is where I want you, daddy," I moaned out as he chuckled and began to attack my clit with precision.

He was eating me so good, my legs started to shake as I started to cum all in his mouth. I watched as Nash leaned back to unbutton his shirt and dropped his pants as I watched him grip his thick penis in hand, and he began to stroke it as I unlatched my bra and threw it to the side. I got on all fours as I crawled to the end of the bed. I opened my mouth wide, and he began to fuck my face. I leaned back a little to grip it with my hands as I spit on the head and brought it to the back of my throat to gag on it a little bit. I leaned down to slip his balls into mouth as I brought my tongue back up the base to the head. I knew he was getting ready to cum as he backed away from me to get himself under control.

"Turn that ass around," he groaned out as I followed exactly what he asked me to do and arched my back with precision at the edge of the bed.

I felt his thick head begging for entry from the back as he began to give me deep, long strokes.

"Ohhh, don't stop!" I moaned out as he continued to stroke me into oblivion.

"Harder. Mmmm, daddy," I cried out as he began to speed up when he abruptly turned me over on my back as he threw my legs over his shoulder to get deeper access.

I could feel him deep in my guts as I heard him groan in my ear as he began to nibble on my ear down to my neck. Getting my pussy more wet the more he continued to go, I continued to cum all over his dick, and he still hadn't cum yet. I didn't know what the hell this man was taking, but I wasn't going to complain not one bit. Nash dropped one of my legs down as he began to slow down his strokes to match the beat of the next song that I hadn't noticed had started.

"Shit!" I heard him groan out as he started to cum. He pulled out to grab a wet rag out the bathroom, and he cleaned the both of us up.

"My bad. I didn't plan for our night to end this way. I wanted to show you this wasn't just about sex. But yo ass had me acting all out of character and shit," he added with a smirk as he got into the bed to lay next to me after throwing the rag back in the bathroom on the sink.

"I don't ever do no shit like that," he added in an afterthought. It was silent for a little while as I just laid there in my thoughts.

"I know you not used to all of this, but I just want the chance to show you not all men are the same. Now, I joke a lot, but if you don't feel this is something you want to do, keep it real with me because there is only so much my ego gon' take, baby. Plus, I'm going to have to stop putting this dick in your life if you don't act right," he added as he smacked my ass playfully.

"I hear you, and I see that already. You didn't have to tell me that. I've just been through so much stuff with men and love in general. I'm just worried about how all of this is going to go when you're on the road for away games and stuff. I've never dealt with that before," I responded as he pulled me into his body and kissed my cheek.

"Just give it one day at a time. Just know I'm going

to give this relationship my all. I'm here to love you and keep you safe. I'm going to do that with every fiber of my being, so let me take the driver seat and enjoy the ride," he responded as I drifted off to sleep with my thoughts.

I just hoped that this time love gave my ass a break, because I was getting tired of coming out on the losing side.

I HAD BEEN DREADING THIS MOMENT EVER SINCE I called her scandalous behind to let her know I was just upset and that I would do what she needed me to do. Today, she had asked me to meet her at her home, which was a beautiful size mansion with modern flares to it. I parked in the front of the house as I made my way to the front door, dreading every step I was taking. The minute I rang the doorbell, I was ready to turn back around and head to my house, but I knew this was something I needed to take care of. The door pulled open with a quickness. This woman was dramatic as hell. She had a full silk robe on with feathers around her neck,

"Please come in, darling," she added in her uppity voice. I rolled my eyes as I stepped into the foyer. This woman was completely horrible. She walked into the living room and had a seat to tell me to have a seat.

"So, what brings you to my home?" she asked like

she wasn't the one who told me to come to her house if I recalled correctly.

"Oh, cut the crap. You know you invited me over here. You also know you screwed me with getting a loan. Now you want me to marry your no-good ass son —" I started as she threw her hand up to stop me from talking like I was a child.

"You ungrateful bitch, I'm trying to help you out, and all you can do is complain. You should be happy that I'm saving you from that hoodlum of a boyfriend that you have now. Just because he is in the NBA doesn't mean he is going to be anything once his tired career is up. So put a smile on your face and get over yourself. Now, I've contacted a wedding planner for your impending nuptials," she started as she placed a binder full of swatches and dinner menus on the table in front of us. This bitch still thought I was marrying her son, but she had another thing coming before I let it get that far.

I swear Lena needed to get this figured out and fast before I became the new Mrs. Jefferson. I just knew this evening couldn't get any worse until I heard her front door open, and in walked Troy with a surprised expression on his face. Probably because I had cursed him out so bad recently, but maybe that will make him snap out of it and just tell his mother that he was gay. That would help out the both of us. He could get his freedom, and I could get my studio free and clear. I watched him catch his expression as it turned into a grin.

"Oh, I didn't know you were going to be over here.

Mom you never told me when you invited me over," he responded as he looked at his appearance like I gave a fuck about what he was wearing.

"Oh, honey I forgot. Why don't you two go out somewhere together?" She started as I started to shake my head trying to come up with other plans because I couldn't be seen anywhere with this man, or it would be back to Bronx in seconds.

"I have to go to my studio to make sure schedules are set for next week. I don't have time to be doing anything extra," I responded with a tight smile, trying to hold back what I really wanted to say in the first place rather than what was coming out of my mouth.

"Oh, please honey, once he becomes your husband, you're going to need to learn he comes first, and your little shop comes second," she added in her usual uppity tone.

"It's a dance studio, and we'll see if that happens," I stated.

"Right, well you two enjoy yourself tonight," she stated in a hard tone.

Letting me know me going out with her son wasn't up for discussion. I was going to keep this as classy as possible because I needed this loan, but I was too ready to cuss her old ass out.

"Let's go, and I'm driving," I grumbled as we made our way outside toward my car.

I didn't know which was worse, being seen in his car or him being seen in my car with me. But I surely wasn't getting ready to find out. I pulled open my door with him getting in the passenger seat.

"So where we going?"

"Just be quiet and sit back," I stated with an attitude while turning the music up to prevent him from
saying one word to me.

Anything this man did disgusted me and just pissed
me off, I knew I needed to let the shit he did to me go,
but something in me couldn't stop me from being petty
as I turned the music back down.

"So how's Erick? Still crying and shit?" I asked as I
stopped at the red light glancing over at him to see he
was getting mad. Shit, I was confused on why his ass
was getting mad. If I recalled correctly, he loved that
crying ass nigga when I walked in on them.

"He cool," he uttered.

"Don't be quiet now. Shit, you were yelling out your
happiness loud and clear that day," I responded.

"Pull this fucking car over, Lavonka," he sneered.

I laughed as I continued to drive because we were
right down the street from our destination anyway.

"Right, we are going to have this date since you and
your mother want it so bad! Plus, we made it to where
we are going!" I responded smartly as I parked the car
in the lot.

"A fucking dog park! You don't even have any
fucking dogs with you to walk, Vonka!" he yelled
irritated.

"I sure do. Get yo' ass out! I think you walk pretty
good," I responded as I parked the car to get out and
headed toward the park not caring whether he came
or not.

I sat down in front of the lake as I watched other

people pass who were walking their dogs. I was just thinking. I was getting so sick of people taking something from me to make themselves whole. What about me? If you continued to take and take, there would soon be nothing left over for me. But did anybody care about that? No. Not until I met Bronx who would give me his last to make sure I was whole, even if he was half full. Not saying that I would let my man become half empty trying to make me happy, because that would make me just like all the people I had come across in my life besides Lena. I forgot the whole reason I was even out here until Troy came and sat next to me with a somber expression as I faced forward, not even acknowledging his presence at first.

"Haven't you taken enough already?" I asked somberly.

"What do you mean?" he asked like he was just so unaware of the shell I had become in our relationship while he was getting his rocks off with a man.

"I mean, not only did you distance yourself in the relationship and made me feel that I was inadequate, but you slept around on me with a man. Now, you want to take the one person from me who cares about me for me. Is the other stuff not enough? What more do you need from me to make yourself happy? Hmm?" I asked as my hard shell of angry words tumbled all around me as tears of every heartbreak I had experienced in my life came at me all at once.

"This isn't about you," he stated flatly as I glanced over his way to see he had tears of his own slowly cascading down his face.

"Well, who is it about?!" I asked as angry tears started to make their way to the forefront. "Because if I see the situation correctly, you know you don't want to be with me, but to keep your devil of a mother happy, you're willing to expense my love and life to make yourself happy," I fumed. He finally turned his head to look me into my eyes.

"Do you really think I'm happy with all of this? It hurt me to hurt you after everything I had done already, but I can't tell my mother one more thing to disappoint her. Having that conversation and telling your only parent who has cared for you her whole life that her son would rather be with a man, you don't know how much it is eating me up to watch the way everything is playing out. I just don't know how to tell her! So I apologize that she has dragged you into this, and that I dragged you into it by going on along with it. I'm going to fix this before it's too late. I swear I just need some time to come to terms with what I'm going to say," he confessed as tears continued to fall down his cheek. I had waited for that apology for forever. Maybe this was all supposed to happen.

I knew God had a plan all along, but I wished he would have gone about it differently. I would have rather had him come by my house and say, "Aye, my bad. I fucked up," and then leave. I would've cried a little bit and then that would be the end. That sounded good, but I knew I probably would have slammed the door in his face before "Aye" would have entirely gotten out of his mouth. A giggle slipped out, causing him to look up at me.

"What's so funny? I'm being real. I'm going to fix this," he asked as I continued to laugh.

"It's not that, but the fact that your butt could have told me all that before I shot your ass! Then, I could have missed out on the heartbreak and got a gay friend out of it!" I stated as I pushed his shoulder watching a smirk come across his handsome face.

"Shit, we can still be cool," he added, smiling up at me with hope in his eyes.

At one time he used to be my best friend, until one day he wasn't anymore. Now, I see that was because he was lost, and he was taking so much from me trying to find himself in me, but I couldn't make him whole even if I wanted to.

"I don't know about all of that. You still left me high and dry, so I'm going to have to think on that." I laughed as he shook his head at me.

"I'm going to try and fix this before your man finds out. I don't need those kind of problems right now," he stated in a serious expression as I burst into laughter.

"Oh, trust me. I know you think we came to the dog park just because I was trying to be funny. Now, that is true, but it's not the only reason! That man doesn't know anybody or step foot toward a dog park." I laughed as he nodded his head.

"Now, tell me about your little boo. I know I was a little mean last time, so I didn't get to know him," I added sweetly as he looked over at me like I was crazy.

"No kidding, I don't think that was the best time to get to know anybody. Plus, you were ready to splatter his and my brains," he responded as I nodded my head in agreement.

"Yeah, you right about that. When you see Lena, if she doesn't fuck you up first, you should thank her. She saved y'all lives, to be honest," I added with a smirk as he started to laugh.

"Oh, I wasn't kidding," I stated as I watched his smile fall a little bit.

"Oh, trust, I know that shit. I ended up in the hospital with a bullet in my ass, remember? I still haven't been able to explain how that happened correctly to my mom," he added with a shake of his head as I smiled back at the memories.

"Good times." Yeah, I know my ass is just a tad bit crazy, but that's how my man liked it, so I didn't give a damn.

"Well, if you think you over me, I would be cool with letting you formally meet him. We going out to the club tonight if you want to bring Lena along with you. It's my first time being to a gay bar," he said with a cocky grin, causing me to burst into laughter.

"Oh, I'm over you, alright. Have you seen my man? And don't say nothing smart. I fight over mine!" I added as we both burst into laughter. I never thought I would see the day where we would be sitting around in a dog park laughing and talking about our men. But life is full of surprises, and you never know what can be in store for you.

"But I'm down. Just text me the time and place," I stated as we hopped up to head back to my car. "Oh yeah, tell your man don't start that crying shit either.

That was so unattractive," I responded with a serious expression. That shit was disgusting watching all that snot dripping down his face like that. Eww, just thinking about it was pissing me off again.

"Aww, man, I told you he was in a high-pressure situation," he responded as we hopped in the car.

"Yeah, aight. If you say so." I laughed.

Later that Night

"I cannot believe I let you convince me to come to a gay club with the ex who you shot in the butt. Just in case you forgot that little detail," Lena complained as we pulled up in front of Score, which was one of the most popping gay clubs in Miami.

"Oh hush, you weren't doing nothing besides sitting by the phone waiting on Nash to call you. I don't know what he did to you on that date, but he definitely got you speaking a new tone, which is fine, because you needed it. Now, suck it up, and have a good time!" I responded as I parked the car.

"Plus, we had a little chit-chat, and I'm over the situation, and so is he," I added while adjusting my boobs in bra, since I decided to go with a see-through shirt and all-black jeans with a nice pair of black stilettos, and I decided to let my natural blonde and black curls down.

While Lena had on an all-red bandage style dress that hugged her body with her hair falling down her back in curls paired with black heels. We were some bad bitches, and we knew it as we walked past the line of people waiting outside because Troy had gotten a table and was waiting for us at the door when we got there. The minute he saw us, he admired our outfits with a smirk and a nod.

"I love those shoes, Lena, and you never used to wear your natural curls. Looks good on you, Vonka." I smiled.

"Thanks, so are we standing out here all night?" I added as he shook his head and walked in to lead us to their table.

I was nervous to meet my ex's boyfriend. That shit sounded ridiculous. I felt a tap on my shoulder.

"Girl, I can't believe we actually here, and don't be mean when we get up there," she whispered like I didn't know how to act.

The minute we reached the table, cry baby hopped up and walked up to us hesitantly like he didn't know if this was a joke or not. "Oh, relax, you not fucking my man anymore, so we cool," I stated bluntly as Lena pushed my shoulder with a smack of her lips.

"She is so rude. I'm Alena, but everyone calls me Lena. Nice to meet you on better terms!" she added in a sweet voice as I looked over at her like she was crazy.

"It's cool, and I know what you mean. Well, I'm Erick, and it's nice to meet y'all too on different levels!" he added in a high-pitched voice.

I looked over at Troy who had stars in his eyes while looking over at Erick, who was talking Lena's ear off. That was what her ass got for being overly friendly. I laughed as everyone looked over at me like I had something.

"Carry on," I stated as I looked out into the crowd, trying to figure out a game plan to get a good drink.

When "Rude Boy" by Rihanna started playing, I hopped up as I started heading for the steps, grabbing Erick and Lena's hand. Nobody couldn't tell me nothing about Rihanna, and this was my song. We got to the middle of the floor as Lena started slow grinding while moving into a slow tick that followed every beat. I followed suit as we began to fuck it up, and to my surprise, Erick was keeping up. Well, shit, who was I kidding? Gay men were always a good time. If he and I hadn't met under previous circumstances, we might have been able to hang out, outside of Troy. I smiled as we all danced until we couldn't dance no more. We started making our way toward the bar when someone shoulder checked me. I looked over my shoulder to notice it was the same females who seemed to pop up everywhere Lena was, and the last couple of times they were saved by an angel, but not today. I was tagging that ass this time, regardless of what Lena was talking about. Before I could finish that thought, Lena walked around me and gripped the girl's hair dragging her back toward us.

"Bitch, is excuse me in your fucking vocabulary? I just keep giving you and ya little friends passes. But that shit is up today," she responded as she began whooping her ass, and what was crazy was this bitch's friends stood back, watching and shaking their heads.

I wish Lena would have done that and a bitch was whooping my ass like she was doing homegirl. I mean, I ain't lost a fight yet, but shit, anything could happen. But Lena would have to catch me with those thangs next, regardless if I ended up getting my ass beat or not. I finally started to feel bad for the girl, so I grabbed Lena around the waist with the help of Erick to pull her off the girl.

"Bitch, try me like this again. Go make yourself useful and keep catching Quran's babies you cum bucket!" she yelled as she kicked her.

I swear this girl was like a Sour Patch Kid. One minute she was happy, and the next she could be sour like a muthafucka. I looked over to see Troy had made his way over to us to get us out the club before more nonsense popped off. The minute I stepped outside, I thanked Troy and Erick for inviting us and let Troy know we needed to figure out this situation with his mother fast as he nodded in agreement. *I didn't know how much he was going to uphold his end of the bargain, but I hoped he did*, I thought as we walked to my car in silence. I was sure she was thinking just as hard I was because tonight had made a turn for the worst quickly. The minute we got in the car and pulled away from the curb, she turned in her seat to look at me as she rubbed her knuckles.

"How in the heck do those females keep bumping into us everywhere we go? I should have asked her that shit before I whooped her ass," she stated, more to herself I was sure than to me.

"That's the real question. Let me find out her dumb ass out here being inspector gadget for Quran," I stated as she looked over at me like she wanted to tell me something but didn't.

"What was that look for?" I asked as we were finally pulling up in front of her house.

"Nothing. I'll talk to you about it later. Goodnight," she responded as she hopped out of the car with a quickness as she headed into her building.

I didn't know what she has going on, but I was going to give her a chance to tell me herself before I figured it out myself. I pulled away from the curb, making my back to my man. Lord knows I needed my booty rubbed after all this nonsense.

BRONX

"VEE, I GOTTA GO!" I GROANED AS SHE BEGAN TO nibble on the corner of my ear, making her way down to my neck.

"I don't want you to go!" she moaned out, trying to turn to me on. She knew the exact way to get me started as I tried to remove myself from her body.

I knew if she kept it up, we would be fuckin' before I left out of this house.

"You gon' be straight. I'll back in a couple days. You can't do this every time I have an away game, baby," I added with a smirk as she looked up at me trying to give me her best set of puppy eyes she could pull off.

I leaned down to kiss her lips as her grip started to loosen up on me, giving me the chance to slip out of her grasp. I rushed to grab my luggage as I made my way to the door and tried to make my way to the front door. I knew she wasn't going to make it to the door as fast as my ass was going because she had tried to go all out wearing little to nothing in the room, and she hated the way the wood floors felt on her feet. So I know she was grabbing her house shoes. The minute I stepped out onto the porch, I heard the screen door open behind me as I power walked over to my car because she just didn't know how to act at all when it came to me leaving the house for away games. I knew that shit wasn't anyone's fault but my own, since I was the one who had spoiled her ass rotten. I felt arms wrapped around my waist as she laid her head against my back.

"I don't want you to go," she mumbled as I threw my gym bag into the back seat.

"I'll call you as soon as we land. Don't worry about it. I got you!" I added with a laugh. I turned around, leaning down to kiss her forehead then her lips.

"Now, get yo' fine ass in the house before someone sees you out here with this skimpy ass robe on!" I added as I smacked her on the ass.

"Don't start nothing that you can't finish." I laughed as I hopped in my truck to head to the airport so we could make it to California.

I finally made it to the airstrip as we all started heading onto the plane to take our seats. I pulled out my phone to text Vee one more time before we took off, because it was my natural superstition that I had to talk to her before I took flight ever since the one time I didn't do that shit, and we almost ended up in the middle of the fucking Pacific. I texted her letting her know I loved her and would call the minute we landed. I saw Nash walk onto the plane with the same stupid ass grin I had on my face. I watched him with a shake of my head as he put his bag in the carry section above my seat as he sat next to me without a word.

"You're a rude ass nigga, man," I stated with a grin as I looked down at my phone, waiting for Vee to text me back.

"Shit, I'm doing the same thing you're doing, wit' yo' hating ass!" he responded with a laugh.

"Yeah, aight. So how the shit you planned go?" I asked as I watched her text finally come back in with a picture of her in just the same robe she had on earlier with nothing on, with the words, "I'll be waiting for you daddy," attached. This that shit I be talking about, which is exactly why I had to make her my wife. I didn't see myself with any other woman.

"Yeah, it was cool. I'm glad her crazy self didn't try and turn that damn carriage around since she didn't know what was up. We going to give this relationship a chance. Well, I convinced her to give it a shot," he added in an excited tone.

"Man, I know I don't have to tell you this, but if you fuck up, you gon' have to see me. That girl has been through too much to experience bullshit at your hands," I added in a no-nonsense tone. He nodded in response because he respected where I was coming from on her situation. Shit, I knew it was like pulling teeth to get her to this point in the first place.

"You ever figure out who has been calling you and hanging up?" he asked.

"Hell nah. I told you I think it's that crazy bitch from that one time I fucked up on Vee," I somberly responded because I just knew if Vee found out about this shit it was going to be game over.

We didn't say shit else for the rest of the plane ride. I couldn't get this situation out of my mind, because the minute I found out who was playing around on my phone, it was definitely going to be a problem.

After the game

We had busted they ass tonight with a seventy-point lead, so I was happy as hell to be going back to my room. The minute I stepped into my room, I ran into an older woman sitting on my bed with an envelope.

"Uh excuse me, ma'am, I think you got the wrong room," I responded in a respectful tone because my mother always taught me to respect my elders.

"Oh, no, son I got the right room. So now I see why she wanted to keep you around. You're a good-looking man with a nice job and manners," she stated with a smirk coming across her face as she stood up to hand me the envelope she had been holding onto when I first came in.

"Who the hell are you, and who is she?" I asked as I sat my gym bag to the side.

"Now, he appears. I always told her you weren't better than my son. He is the better man for Lavonka, and I'm going to make sure that happens," she added snidely.

"You don't know shit about my relationship, and who is your son?" I asked, getting pissed off but not showing one trace of agitation, which I could tell was irritating her. She ignored my question and proceeded to place the envelope in my hand.

"What the hell is this?" I asked as I looked down at the envelope she placed into my hand while heading toward the door.

She looked over her shoulder and said, "It's the end," as she walked out of the room leaving questions and confusion behind her as I debated whether or not to open the envelope or not. Did I really want to know what was going on? Shit, was there even anything for me to be concerned with was what worried me? I laid the envelope on the side table as I headed into the bathroom to wash away all the dirt and grime from the night. The minute I stepped back into the room, the first thing my eyes latched onto was that white envelope. I tightened the towel around my waist as I leaned down to open the envelope. I couldn't waste another moment. I didn't know what the hell was in this shit, but I surely was going to find out as I popped the back open, and instantly my phone started ringing. I knew it couldn't be anyone except Vee calling me at this time of night as I placed the envelope back on the side table to answer the phone.

"What you over there doing? What happened to you calling me as soon as you got in the room?" she yelled as I let a chuckle slip because she was crazy as hell. I knew she probably assumed I had another female in here.

"I can't wash my ass, baby?" I asked, trying to be smart.

"Nah, I want you dirty and all! You could have

called me on FaceTime, so I can make sure ain't no bitches trying to hop in the shower with you," she added with a smack of her teeth.

"Here you go with this nonsense again, I don't have no other woman in this damn room. You think I really need that when I got you here driving my ass crazy? I don't need two. You're more than enough, baby," I added in a serious tone.

"You're still fresh out the shower?" she asked in a sultry tone. I knew she was getting ready to be on shit.

"Mmmhmm, what you got on?" I asked as I plopped down on my bed.

"Call me on FaceTime and find out!" she added as I hung up instantly to call her back on FaceTime. The minute she answered the phone, I could see it was pitch black in the room.

"Vee turn the damn lights on. How am I gonna see any damn thing?" I yelled out in frustration.

"Relax, we getting there, slow and steady wins the race, baby," she responded to the sounds of "It Seems Like You're Ready" by R. Kelly started playing. That's when the lights began to dim out. I licked my lips as she walked back into view of the camera with the same silk short pink robe she had on in the picture as I started to remove my towel. I watched as she began to make slow and sultry moves as she let her robe drop at her feet. She had on a black lace bra with matching thongs and a garter belt on her thighs. I watched as she began to rub on her breast as I propped my leg up to whip my shit out. I watched as she bit her bottom lip while grinding her hips in a slow, sultry motion as she dropped down to drag her hand down between her breasts and between her legs. She came back up as she continued to dance as she turned her back toward me and unlatched her bra and letting it fall into the pile with her panties not too far behind.

"Let me see you stroke it, daddy." I heard her moan out as took her two fingers and slipped them into her mouth just to watch her drag those same fingers down her body and in between her thighs as she began to play with her clit, causing my dick to become instantly hard as I ran my hands in the same fashion she was touching herself as she moaned out and took her fingers from in between her legs and slipped them back into her mouth.

"How that shit taste, baby? I can taste you on the tip of my tongue," I groaned out as I felt myself reaching my nut.

I watched as she brought her hands back in between her legs and inserted two fingers as she went to town moaning out my name bringing herself to a peak as I watched her cum so beautifully. I couldn't hold back anymore. I rushed to grab my towel before I nutted all over the bed. I didn't have any intentions of calling a maid to change these damn sheets.

"Shit, you're just full of surprises," I stated as I watched her grab her robe up to put back on as she picked the phone up to start a bath.

"I only do it for you, baby," she added over her shoulder since she had propped the phone up on the counter and started throwing all types of shit in the tub. I was assuming to make bubbles. I watched as she dropped her robe to lay back into the water. "So how was your day today, baby?" I asked as she looked over at me sleepily.

"Exhausting, I just wanted to be with you, but I handled some things with the studio." She smiled. I was so happy that she had that studio because, although she had been pretty stressed, I still knew this was what she had been dreaming of her entire life.

I offered to pay for the studio, but she didn't want my money. Her exact words were that she wanted to figure it out on her own. Shit, I couldn't do nothing but respect the fact that she didn't want a handout, which it wouldn't have been that way to me, but that's the way she saw it. I thought back to that envelope that I had still sitting on my side table half open.

"Hey, Vee, you ain't got shit to tell me that I need to know, do you?" I asked as she looked back over at me with squinted eyes,

"No, nothing new is going on. Why?" she asked as I thought about mentioning the woman who was in here earlier, but for some reason, I just decided against it.

If she says nothing is new, I believed her, so I shouldn't be surprised or worried by shit I saw in that envelope. So I walked over to the end table to grab the envelope.

"What's that?" she asked as I pulled the latch back to pull out a note and a stack of pictures.

"Just some envelope a woman gave me today." I pulled the letter first that read:

Love is a funny thing, it's incredible how much you think you know about your partner. Isn't it?

I turned over the pictures to see Vee's ass at the park with a whole other nigga, hugged up and shit. I kept flipping through the photographs seeing them in the car together and on dinner dates with that old bitch that was just in here. Acting like they were a happy ass family. I kept flipping through until I made it to the last card that was placed in the envelope. It looked like a wedding invitation that said:

You are formally invited to the union of Troy Robinson & Lavonka Jenkins. Please R.S.V.P. if you plan to attend on 06/10/2018.

I couldn't take more. I wanted to fuck her up so bad because she had my ass out here looking stupid as fuck. I was out here worried about making sure her insecure ass was secure in her feelings for me. Calling when she needed me to, just to make sure I kept her happy because this was supposed to be our damn wedding invitation. But she had already traded up on me and went back to a muthafucka who she claimed was gay, but I guess that shit was a lie too. I felt a tear slide down my cheek as I quickly wiped it away.

"What's the problem, baby? Are you okay?" she asked in that smooth voice that always caused me to become calm, but today, at this moment, it felt different.

"Aye, have yo' shit out my spot by the time I get back. I ain't the one to fuck with, so keep that crazy shit you do to yourself. Don't let me get back and you've fucked up my shit. Oh yeah, congratulations on the wedding," I added as I put the wedding invitation on the screen.

While hanging up before she could get another word out. I gave her the chance to let me know what was up, but she couldn't do that shit. She sat in that fucking tub and lied to my face like I didn't mean shit to her. This was exactly why I didn't fuck with relationships, but when I saw her, I just knew she was meant for me, but maybe my damn senses are off. I threw the stack of pictures and invitations across the room with enough force to knock the lamp off the stand. I pulled on my sweatpants as I headed out the room to make my way outside. I just needed to get away. I made it out the doors of the lobby but decided to take the back way to avoid fans and shit. I just didn't feel the need to talk with anybody as I instantly felt something extremely hard hit me upside my head. The last words I heard as my body was being lifted were, "Where the hell are we taking him? He ain't no regular ass nigga, Ma!" I didn't know who was fucking with me right now, but the minute I woke up, they were going to figure out exactly why I went to Bronx.

I DIDN'T KNOW WHERE I WENT WRONG AS I WATCHED his face contort in confusion as he went through every picture. I didn't know how the hell he got those, but he could have fucking asked me before assuming that what he saw in those damn pictures was what it seemed. I pulled myself out of the tub as I began to call his phone back to back. I was trying to receive a call back just so I could explain what really happened. But his phone continued to go straight to voicemail, I was not sure if his petty ass blocked my number or if he had his phone off. But this shit wasn't funny, and I wasn't going anywhere until he brought his ass back here and we talked this through like adults. All I kept replaying through my head was him asking me if there was anything he needed to know. I knew I should have said something right then and there, but who knew that the one thing that could ruin our entire relationship was within that damn envelope. I screamed out as I called Lena, who picked up on the second ring huffing like she had been running miles or some shit. "Bitch, why you sound like you been running a damn marathon?" I asked.

"No reason, make it quick, Vee. I know you wouldn't call this late unless it was important, and Nash is on the other line," she huffed out. This bitch was over there doing the same shit I was doing earlier. You get real good at phone sex when you have a man that's always away at away games.

"Bronx found out about Troy. Told my ass to pack up and be gone by the time he got back," I admitted.

"Well, hold for one brief moment," she added. I guess this bitch thought she clicked over when she started talking again.

"Babe, you're gonna have to put it up, and I'll show you a little something later. Vonka on the other—" I stopped her right there.

"Y'all nasty, and I'm still on the phone." I laughed.

"Mind yo' business. Hold on one more time." She laughed as the phone went quiet. I guess she got it figured out that she was on the wrong damn line in the first place. It had been about ten minutes, and I was getting ready to hang up and call her again because I didn't wait on hold.

"Hello, so start from the beginning. How the hell did he find out?" she asked as I plopped down on the bed to tell her how it all happened in the first place.

"Damn, so he hasn't been answering the phone at all?" she asked.

"No, he hasn't been answering. I don't know what he thinks this is, but I guess I'm going to be making a trip to L.A., because he doesn't get to leave me without me giving him a response on what the hell is going on!" I yelled as a few tears begun to stream down my cheek.

"You know I'm not letting you leave without me, so get two tickets. When are we leaving?" she asked as a smile came across my face because I didn't think I could have made it on this trip without her.

I'd never found myself in this situation where I needed to prove to him that this wasn't what it seemed. This kind of vulnerability was new to me, and I could tell you this I didn't like the shit.

"Tonight. I'm booking our flights now, so get packed and get over here," I responded as we said our goodbyes.

I ran to my closet to grab my suitcase when I heard my phone start ringing. I ran to pick it up, thinking that Bronx had finally come to his senses to just ask me what was going on. I picked up the phone to be somewhat surprised.

"Bronx, why haven't you been answering my phone calls?" I yelled. When I heard a laugh resound throughout the phone.

"Nope, guess again, hun. I thought I told you to cut that off?" I heard Mrs. Robinson state in a conde-scending tone.

"Well, we can't get everything we want, now can we?" I asked. I was getting sick of this old bitch. Was it really this serious to get your son married off?

"I see you don't listen, so I went ahead and made sure you could hear me loud and clear. Also, did you get my gift I left you on the doorstep?" she asked as I dropped my bag, I thought she was crazy, but damn she was taking all of this pretty far.

"What did you do? You made sure Bronx got those pictures, didn't you?" I mumbled as tears out of pure anger begun to swim down my cheeks.

I was getting tired of people feeling as if I was the one to fuck with because I wasn't, especially when pushed to the limit.

"Oh, hun, that was free of charge! I'm talking about the gift outside of your door. Now once you get over your pity party, we have a cake tasting on Thursday and don't be late, or you will regret it," she vowed while hanging up in the same breath as I let my phone fall from fingers as it hit the bed.

I took slow steps toward the door as it continued to ring over and over again. I looked through the peep-hole to see it was jet black on the other side. I went over to the couch to grab my gun from underneath the couch because I was getting tired of being fucked without my permission! I cocked my gun as I yelled, "Who is it," without getting a response. I pulled open the door to come face to face with a woman and a baby. I had never seen her before as I brought my gun down for a brief moment.

"How can I help you?" I asked as she looked taken back by me answering the door in the first place like she was expecting someone else to get the door.

"Umm, I'm looking for Bronx. Is he home?" she asked with an attitude as she switched the baby carrier from one hand to the other.

I didn't know who this bitch thought she was, but I was not even going to comment on that.

"Umm. he is out of town. How the fuck do you know my man?" I asked, trying to keep my anger at bay since there was a baby cooing no less than a few inches from me.

"I'm coming to let him know he has a child to take care of, and that I'm doing this anymore! I won't be a secret a second longer," she responded with her hand on her hip.

I laughed, catching her completely off guard as I turned around to go back in my house without another word as I shut the door in her face. I heard the doorbell continue to ring as I made my way up the stairs to pack a couple more things into my bag. Not only was I still going to L.A., but when I got to that bitch, I was going to kill this nigga in the process. But I was going to give his ass all of five minutes to explain, unlike he did for me, because I was sweet like that, but if I felt like I was not getting the right answer, he could kiss his little career goodbye once I was done. I laughed as I dragged my suitcase down the stairs and grabbed my car keys to head outside, hoping this deranged hoe wasn't still outside. I walked out to see there was a white envelope with a baby carrier on the porch. I dropped my bag next to the carrier.

"I know this deadbeat ass hoe didn't leave her baby!" I groaned out to myself. I lifted the coverall from the to see there was a note placed on the baby with her birth certificate and a paper where she signed her rights away to the little girl.

I read the sheet to see it said her name was Aimee Benjamin. Not only did she leave this pretty little girl, but she had the nerve to give her my man's last name.

"Lord, let me pray, because I was ready to kill this man on the spot without a second of explanation as I looked down at the sleeping baby, who was a casualty in a big scheme of nonsense. I locked the front door to pick up the carrier as I realized I had forgotten all about the other envelope. So I picked that up and headed toward the truck to buckle her carrier into the back seat as I opened the envelope with pictures of Bronx tied up and knocked out with a gun to his head, and the note read:

If you want him to live, do not contact him anymore, because if you do, he surely won't be able to reach you.

Love, Mom.

I don't know what the fuck was wrong with this woman, but she took it entirely too far this time, I thought as I parked the car and unhooked the baby's carrier to bring it back into the house because this situation was going to take more finesse than just taking a plane down to L.A. in search of someone I probably would never find without help. This day just couldn't get any fucking worse! I pulled my phone out to give Lena a call because we were going to have to go about this a whole different way.

"It's about time we come the fuck out of retirement. I'm tired of people taking us for a joke."

To be continued…

I WON'T
Count To
LOVE
AGAIN
2

IESHA BREE

Check Out My Catalog

If you enjoyed I Won't Lose to Love Again and want to read any of my other work, check out this list of my novels and novellas. You will not be sorry!

Novels & Novellas

Envy: Mae Sisters Series (Can be read as a standalone, and Series) – Romance

Rush: Mae Sisters Series (Can be read as a standalone, and Series) – Romance

Hope: Mae Sisters Series (Can be read as a standalone, and Series) – Romance

Deception: Mae Sisters Series (Can be read as a standalone, and Series) – Romance/Urban Fiction

The Love You Bring (Standalone) – Romance

Unlove Me (Standalone) - Romance

EX I Don't Want to Be (Standalone) - Romance

The Love Pledge (Standalone) – Romance

Anthology

Payback Get 'em Back Like That (Anthology – Even the Score) – Urban Fiction

Check my website www.ieshabree.com to stay up to date on

character updates, sneak peeks, and Lifestyle Post! Also, get your paperbacks from this website as well!

Get Connected!

PENNING SMOOTH MEN TO MEND BROKEN HEARTS

Have you signed up yet?! If not, what are you waiting for? Click this link to become a part of my book club! We're a group of amazing readers & authors who love to talk books! We look forward to having you apart of the Family!

Love My Way w/ Iesha Bree : https://www.facebook.com/groups/2236965113006971/?ref=share

CPSIA information can be obtained
at www.ICGtesting.com
Printed in the USA
LVHW090136071120
670844LV00014B/520